# Truth Be Told

## Claire Goff

# Dedication

For my mum, my son and my dear daughter. Thank you for your never-ending faith in me. Xxx

# One

'Mum. Muuummm. Oh my god! Mummmmmm ... Mum hurry ... Please Mummmmmmmm!'

That, may I say, was what I woke up to at 4am this morning, the screams of my thirteen-year-old daughter. It is the year 2010, the 24th of March, a day that one will never forget. Sadie is my only child and by the sounds of it she was just about to have a child of her own. Statistically, I guess I shouldn't have expected anything else considering the fact that my mum, my aunt, myself and pretty much most of the women around me have had our babies young, and all ended up at some point becoming just another single parent. But hey ho, off to work we go. As my nan once said, there's no time for tears, and this was one of those times. So the devastation and fear that I feel for my baby girl right now must be temporarily masked. I have to be the strong one, nothing new there I guess. So first things first, I need to get the baby bag.

'Aaaaaahhh it hurts so bad, Mum,' wailed Sadie again.

'Ok darling, deep breaths. Mum's just getting your bag.' I try to sound calm.

'Ewwwwwwwww I think I've wet myself,' cried Sadie.

'Oh it's probably just your waters, baby girl. Stay there I'll grab your joggers.' I respond in a soothing tone. Shit where did I put that bag? Oh fuck, think Kate, where's the baby bag? Yes I remember I put it in the bottom of the wardrobe. The wardrobe reminded me of the wardrobe from the movie, *The Lion, The Witch and The Wardrobe*, it is humongous. I spotted the battered old piece at a second-hand shop in Rochester a few weeks ago and thought with a little bit of tlc it would be great for the baby's room.

Rochester is my most favourite place in the Medway towns and whenever anyone new asked where it was that I came from it was Rochester that fell from my lips rather than Chatham. Chatham really is the Peckham of Medway. Like the wardrobe was probably far too grand for such a small room, Rochester was far too grand for Medway. I just couldn't resist the over the top purchase, for just fifty pounds I didn't even have the audacity to barter and I really couldn't complain it was a solid antique pine wardrobe worth at least three hundred pounds. And unlike an Argos wardrobe my wardrobe has a history and I'm most certain it will also have a much longer shelf life than that of the mass production wardrobes that so many of us are forced to purchase because they are cheap and cheerful but also broken within a year. One does love Rochester.

Surprisingly Sadie even ended up helping me with the rubbing down, and then together we colour washed the gigantic piece in white, and much to Sadie's dismay it looked great, especially against the new white cot and chest of drawers that my mum had bought as a gift for the baby. All that was left to get now was a new blind, but Sadie insisted that we wait until the baby arrived because the sex of the baby determined the colour of the blind. My little girl wants baby blue for a boy and baby pink for a girl. The shock that my own little dolly is going to have her own baby still hits me like a big fat kick in the stomach, it literally takes my breath away certainly when she makes childish requests like that of the blind. It seems today is the day that we can decide on the colour of the blind. Today of all days, the 24th of March, a day I once cursed, why today? I will never know, maybe this was just another cruel joke sent from the universe.

'Ok baby we're nearly there, just a couple more minutes now, deep breaths darling. Yes that's it. Breathe in and out,' I say, trying to sound reassuring whilst praying my clapped out Clio makes it to the hospital!

For just a small nanosecond of a moment I lose myself in my own thoughts, my wishful thoughts, away from the now, the dreaded reality. We were travelling to France via the boat, just like the few times before when we had managed to get a *Sun* break for a fiver and my poor baby Sadie had experienced sea sickness and I was telling her to breathe, deep breaths! However this wasn't France and my soothing and reassuring tone wasn't cutting it and it certainly didn't seem to stop the temporary Tourette's syndrome that my daughter had adopted throughout the whole journey to the hospital. Well actually for the entire labour. It seemed Sadie had turned into something that replicated a scene from *The Exorcist*. But in all fairness Sadie is only just thirteen and still a child and she isn't having the easiest of labours.

Eventually after a very emotional and physically exhausting nineteen hours Sadie managed to push another little lady out into this world. Still the 24$^{th}$ of March lingers on. I am so proud but at the same time so scared. Not only am I the sole provider for Sadie now it seems I am gaining another single load. Jesus what was this society coming to? Talk about the lost generation. Where have all the decent men gone? The once upon a time chivalrous providers!

Both my precious little girl and my beautiful granddaughter were peacefully sleeping for now. How, I'll never know. It's not exactly quiet in here, what with the drumming and the buzzing from the strip lights and the various bleeping from the machines that seem to be scattered here there and everywhere, let alone all the other newborns that seem to be crying every five minutes. But here they are both blissfully sleeping and unaware of all there is to come. This turns my mind to another blissfully unaware young boy out there somewhere. I feel a sense of history repeating itself. The memories of Sadie's own father and the lies I have construed are once again evoked. I feel physically sick, already the bile is tossing with my tonsils at the thought of Sadie ever discovering the truth about her so-called dead daddy.

Why Sadie won't disclose the identity of the father I just don't know, surely he couldn't be that bad. Well, I guess, or at least hope, she will eventually tell me. I don't like to push her but I think I'll have to tread carefully and slowly with this one, given her previous mental outbursts whenever I've touched on the whole 'who's the daddy?' subject she completely loses control, hurls abuse at me and then cries uncontrollably. This reaction worries me to my core, why does she react in such an over the top manner? Sadie has always been so dramatic. So I think it best to let her tell me when she's ready. I have even wondered whether my baby had been a subject of rape. I asked her in a subtle way, not direct or blunt, something along the lines of 'no one made you do anything you didn't want to, did they?' Sadie point blank said 'no'. I won't ever give up on the subject, but for now I will let sleeping dogs lie and just enjoy this special and unforgettable moment.

The baby is absolutely beautiful, she is rather intriguing, she has big almond-shaped eyes, a deep and dark pearly green colour which contrasts perfectly against her china-like delicate skin and her bright red copper hair. She is absolutely perfect. She reminds me of my own mother in a funny sort of way. My mother has pale skin and green eyes, just not the copper hair. The baby looks nothing like Sadie. Sadie is kind of Spanish-looking, she has lovely dark skin, masses of dark brown hair and big chocolate brown eyes. Many people often comment on how Sadie looks just like myself, however, if they knew who her father was they would certainly see the striking resemblance is his and not mine. Sadie is most certainly the spitting image of her male maker.

'Hot drink?' whispered a little plump, curly red-haired nurse in a burly thick Scottish accent, interrupting my wandering mind. She was peeping at me from behind the curtain waiting for a reply. Deep in thought my reaction was slightly delayed.

'No, no, I'm absolutely fine thank you. I think I'm going to get off shortly, I was just watching my innocent pair sleeping and thinking about how crazy life can be.'

My own voice sounded so croaky. I felt the lump quickly fill my throat and the tears without warning were already flowing from my ever so tired eyes. Why was I so emotional? I apologise for my unnecessary tears. I think if I were honest with myself this is just one of those times when the loneliness creeps up on you, unexpectedly sucking you into the deep dark hole of despair. You become a sliver of the person you normally are. That's another big thing in the world of being a single parent, the aloneness, the separateness, and the disconnectedness, consumes not only the mind but also the body, leaving you feeling encompassed in worthlessness.

The nurse stroked my arm affectionately and responded, 'Aye they are both very lucky, hen. They are in good hands and thank the lord they're both healthy and well! You should get yerself off home, hen, go and get yerself some rest, God knows you'll need it my gal.'

My body felt so much from the stranger's touch, my

whole sensory system seemed to react to this caring unfamiliar gentle gesture. The thing is when you very rarely get touched by another person you become so very aware of how intense and how sensitive our senses

really are. However this is only emphasised when our bodies are sent into a temporary or a long-term redundancy, as such.

The kind nurse was a little roundish lady of about sixty, she seemed so wise and knowing. It was as if this lady had a sixth sense into my world and an insight into my despair and in a spiritual wisdom kind of way she highlighted my very own seclusion but oddly she also allowed me some hope. The Scottish have always intrigued me. Probably because my great grandfather was Scottish, sadly he died when I was just a baby, so unfortunately I don't even remember him. Apparently he was the last man in our family that provided for his family. All the rest ran and never looked back and consequently we are now left with a bunch of Mads. The term 'Mads' is a joke word often used among myself and my friends as we are both mum and dad combined, just take the first letter of each word and you got m.a.d. Being a m.a.d has also left us mummies slightly frazzled, and what some would describe as mad, hence our birth of the word Mads. The thought of my own daughter becoming a 'Mad' somewhat saddens me, I just hope and pray the young boy responsible for this eventually identifies himself and steps up to his responsibility.

## TWO

As I got closer to my house I noticed it had been decorated abundantly in pink 'new baby girl' banners and balloons. I imagined this was the work of my two neighbours, Frankie and Fiona. I lived in the middle of the pair. Frankie, like me, had her first baby at the age of sixteen. She has another two now, all boys. William Junior, known as Will J, who is now twenty-three, John Boy is twelve and baby Josh is just six months. Frankie's so-called boyfriend and father of her boys is a wide boy called William White. Frankie absolutely loves 'her Willy' as she puts it. She really is completely besotted with him, a true example of blind love. Personally I think William is a nasty drug dealing dirty wrong'un and that would be a polite way of describing him. I've lost count of the times the police bang Frank's door in because of him.

Frank recently caught her Willy shopping in Marks and Spencer with his young plaything. Frank said the girl was barely out of college. Frank attacked the pair of them. Will Snr protected his little plaything and let Frank kick shit out of him. She broke his nose and blackened both his eyes. Frank said she saw them pursuing the frozen food aisle so she picked up a frozen duck and smashed it straight in his face. Frankie is a vicious one. Still she took him back, she will never leave him. Fuck that life. My mum and my Auntie

Joan were the same, both seemed to fall for men that would control and batter them. I'll never get it myself.

My childhood was blighted with many violent alcoholic sniff heads. I swore I would never let that shit into my life and certainly not my children's, love or no love. My mother lived for a faulty man and often moved them in with us, hence my first-hand experience and absolute disdain for violent abusive men. I remember one boyfriend of my mother's, Ernie was his name. I don't recall his surname and she probably didn't even know this herself.

One night when I must have been around the age of ten I had a friend over to stay. Everything seemed perfectly fine while we were downstairs with Ernie and my mum. Ernie even bought us a takeaway and seemed in good spirits. However this soon changed. The gruelling violence that my mother suffered that night happened after my friend and I went to bed. I can remember waking with a start in the early hours to the screeching sirens and tones of flashing blue lights illuminating my bedroom walls, I knew instantly something serious had gone down. There were police everywhere. The luminosities alone made you very aware that there was an emergency taking place outside. I slowly slipped from my bed and crept over to the window and saw the ambulance carrying my mother out on a stretcher. She was lifeless on the stretcher and in that moment I thought she was dead. The next thing I knew, the police were indoors and in my room asking me if I had anyone I could call as there had been an incident. I later found out that

Ernie had just turned on Mum for no reason whatsoever. Obviously I realise now that he must have had some very severe mental health issues or he was just off his nut from his alcohol and cocaine abuse. My mother was in hospital for six weeks. She ended up with a bleed on the brain, several broken ribs and a fractured jaw, a punctured lung and various bruising. The day she was released from her hospital bed she fell straight back into his vehemently violent arms. Obviously she never learnt. Her weakness and inability to learn and my inability to help her see another way angered and frustrated me. Personally I would rather carry on being a sexually deprived crazy creature who depends on herself and only herself, even to the point of orgasm, rather than succumb to a variety of abuse for the sake of a meaningless fuck and a false sense of security. It's funny really how we juggle and struggle to the point of complete and utter breakage.

Basically I, Kate Andrews, am a 'nearly' thirty-year-old 'single mumma' who like many others in our day and age have been forced to accept that our reality exists on a never-ending merry go round restricted and dominated by the; minimum fucking wage, the scraps of shit support we have to degrade ourselves and beg our system for, school-runs, homework, cooking, scraping enough money together to put food on our tables to nourish our growing babies, washing, cleaning our homes and any others that will throw a few quid our way to make their plush lives easier, ironing, gardening, window cleaning; decorating; oh yeah let's not forget the dutiful bin lady and any other odd job or burden that is chucked our way, and not forgetting the daily grind and stress of keeping our home warm, the water turned on, enough on the electricity account so we can have light at night, and the ultimate daily decisions of whether to spend the last of our shit pile of pennies on either washing powder to keep our clothes clean or toilet paper to wipe our arses as some days we cannot afford to buy both. Oh and believe me it doesn't end there as all of this is then whirl-winded with; final reminders, breakdowns, bank charges, and let's not forgot the gruelling guilt of not really being able to make up for that missing father figure. I know in my heart I am not alone out there but somehow I feel so alone. Gosh I never thought at fifteen this would be where I ended up! How many of you can really relate to my unconscious predictable fate?

My relief, my respite, my sole moments of frustrated release come very rarely and on the odd occasion when you get to jump off the mind-numbing existence of the merry-go-round and you find a break in the madness, a lone fifteen minutes of solitude to indulge in a personal fondle and play in that precise moment of a gushing orgasm all the wretched wench duties are temporarily washed away. Wow the overwhelming relief that is felt for both the body and the mind is sensational. Normally this is well long overdue. The constant throbbing felt from my unpleasured little box finally feels a sense of liberation. It's like a crazy build-up of repressed passion and an intense anger towards the lack of fresh ripe fruits that are on offer, as such. However the sexual tension that has been simmering for some time is momentarily satisfied.

Although I must say that the closeness and intensity of two bodies being wrapped together as one, the mixing of the love juices and the deep intimate connection that is felt both physically and emotionally between lovers is certainly not comparable when it comes to stimulating a natural human sexual desire by oneself. However when you assess what is on offer, it really is a no brainer, a lonely orgasm does not cause you half as much mess and pain as an over-loved cock can. Therefore it looks as if it's the lonely orgasm for me for the duration.

In all fairness I actually have the house to myself for once. I guess I should be making the most of it. The famous Ann Summers wins again thank fuck for the ever so popular vibrating rubber rampant rabbit, as my only other alternative is a married man or a cocaine-addicted self-absorbed womaniser. See that's my problem I would rather go it alone in all my glory than settle for the half-arsed options available to me.

Just as I was about to climb the stairs to bed there was a little tap on the door. It was my neighbour Fiona. I could tell straight away by her silhouette which was visible through the front door. I let her in.

'Hi, my babe. How's them babies?' slurred Fiona. Fiona

had a really strong cockney accent and wine always permeated from her breath. A beautiful woman is Fiona James, voluptuous and curvy in all the right places. She has a heart of gold and a temper so ferocious even the men in our local pubs won't mess with her. In our neighbourhood, Fi-Fi is Fiona's nickname. It's funny really, there is actually a story as to why she is known as Fi-Fi. Basically Fi-Fi is like our very own Robin Hood of Weeds Wood and if it weren't for our Fi-Fi half of us that live on this estate would have probably starved. See the thing is Fi-Fi can get her hands on pretty much anything from coffee to steak, candles to flooring and all at half the price of the stores. Where we come from, this is what you would describe as a big fat bonus.

It's wrong, it's thieving but in a mad crazy arse way, you can kind of justify it, the supermarket giant capitalists shouldn't be so greedy, it's not like she's robbing people's homes. In effect, she's like our old Disney friend Robin Hood 'stealing from the greedy for the sake of the needy!'. And not just those that are on benefits but also those who graft away for a pittance and yet are still forced to live in poverty, on the edge of society, it's income-related, and it's bullshit! High-five our Fi-Fis of the world.

Poor Fi has had no luck with men either, fifty years old, two kids, and neither father was ever involved. Her son, Tom Crane, is a couple of years older than me and he owns his own garage down at the back of Luton Arches. Now that is one naughty area of Chatham. It was only recently that an old lady was discovered butchered to death, cut up into pieces and put in one of the freezers in one of the convenience stores, by the owner. Scary place! I wouldn't walk there in broad daylight let alone at night. You wouldn't believe the deadly creatures that exist in the glorious garden of England!

Tom is brave and I guess he is a bit of a face in Chatham so he doesn't have to worry about deadly creatures. I imagine a family-owned business is a good face for how he really makes his money. A complete mummy's boy is Tom, although he does what he does, he always looks after Fiona. Tom buys her cars and pays for everything, from holidays to her whole house being gutted and completely refurbished, always professionally and to the very highest of standards. Fi's home interior looks like that of a luxury five-star hotel. Fi had been married to a guy called Jonny James for years. He was a right wannabe gangster from London, told the world he was a runner for a couple of known notorious criminals of his time. Fiona told me his so-called 'crim pals' were convicted of raping both little boys and girls. Eventually the sick duo pervert brothers were murdered whilst they were in prison back in the late eighties. Clearly if this was the case, Jonny James would have been effectively shouting to the world he was a nonce too. It was like Tom was proud of his predator pals. My advice to all nonces, don't be fucking proud! Hang your fucking head in shame!

Jesus, Jonny James was the type of bloke that had done,

seen and experienced everything, completely full of shit Jonny James was. Fiona and Jonny were together a good twenty years before he ended up running off with Fiona's twenty-one-year-old daughter, Scarlett. Johnny had brought Scarlett up as his own daughter from around the age of nine months. Say no more about his noncey wannabe gangster pals and his own ancestral incest infected roots.

Fiona has not seen either of them since she caught them in bed together, which was about two years ago. I often wonder if Tom ever got revenge and hushed it up or if he is still on the road to retribution? One thing I definitely know about Tom Crane is that he isn't the type of man that would take that 'incesty' shit lying down. He once told me he would cut his sister's throat and Jonny James would be tortured very slowly if he ever got his hands on them.

Tom is the sort of guy that does not speak unless it's absolutely necessary and when he does, those words that he has carefully chosen are truly intended. A no bullshit man, a good strong loyal man but just bare ugly. Like pale freckly skin, ginger, well a balding ginge, not a tooth in his head or if he has they are black, obviously a common sign of a long-term coke indulger, with a kind of Shrek-looking face. Shame, as Tom Crane would make a great partner, if I were blind. Oh Jesus, I am such a bitch. Anyway bottom line is Tom Crane adores his mum and will clearly kill for her pain.

Fi has a tendency to get drunk and cry for hours about her

unfortunate history with men and how she raised a slag, she certainly has a way with words does our Fiona. I have a feeling this was one of those times.

Fiona was chatting about Sadie and her new baby girl and then out of nowhere she then started muttering about her own baby girl Scarlett and how 'she had grown into a scummy little whore and she hopes that for Sadie's sake her baby girl won't grow up and become a rotten little sket like Scarlett.' Jeez I was so glad Sadie was not here. I'm sure she would have took what Fi was saying to heart and probably screamed merry hell at her.

I rinsed our mugs out, then I locked the back door and I kind of hoped Fiona was getting the hint that I was whacked. I checked my mobile, now the battery had charged, it was on silent and buzzing off the hook. I made sure there was nothing from the hospital and I deliberately ignored the rest. I was far too tired to reply to anyone now. Fiona was falling asleep, wobbling away on the chair.

I shouted, 'Come on Fi let's get you home love.' Not that she took a blind bit of notice of me. I gently lifted her arm and kind of nudged her to get up. She was so wobbly, at one point she nearly pulled me over, just getting her to the front door seemed an adventure in itself.

'Love ya my babe more than you know,' slurred Fi as she staggered up the garden path.

# Three

Will J had been yet again arrested, this time he got caught with his trousers down in his dad's car getting a blow-job from a prostitute on New Road, a place notoriously known for heroin-addicted hookers.

The boy has no driving licence, a big stash of crack and heroin in the boot, five thousand pounds in cash and the plonker was on license for an armed robbery that he had committed a few years earlier. Consequently, this meant Will J was looking at being instantly remanded back to jail. He's not even been out a year. Silly boy and all for a willy lick. Although Will J White liked people to think he was just like his father, he was actually worse than his father could ever be. Will J was into every drug that he could get his grubby little hands on. Whilst in his teens everyone just assumed he was a tearaway like his father, but all said and done regarding big William White being a raging womanising sniff head, he was never into crack and heroin, unlike his firstborn. Not that I think any is better but the detrimental effects that crack and heroin have on a life seem incomparable to that of a recreational cocaine user. This I believe is due to the fact that the majority of cocaine users normally hold down employment and continue with their responsibilities albeit in a massively dysfunctional manner. But compare that to a crack or heroin addict whose life becomes completely controlled by their addiction and their only function is for their next fix and how they are going to pay for it, the two really are worlds apart. My point is a cocaine user is not normally destined to be in and out of prison and regularly facing the death sentence through drug overdoses unlike that of a crack-heroin addict. Will J hid his habit well. Although Frankie and big Will did suspect he experimented at his raves, I don't think that they ever actually realised to what extent.

Frankie and William Snr only realised that their son was dealing in crack and heroin when the police busted open their front door with a search warrant earlier today. It was all going on just as I pulled up outside with Sadie and the baby. Jesus it was like someone had been murdered, two meat wagons and three 'boys in blue' cars, I was worried at first. My immediate thought was that William Snr had hurt Frankie. I don't know why I thought that as William White was a lot of things, however, I have never known him to be a man to hit a woman. As quickly as I had that thought I could hear Frank screaming at the police and instantly I knew she was fine. It was a normal and regular occurrence for the police to come through William and Frank's front door. Even the neighbours didn't seem to come out anymore.

As soon as the last police car was out of sight Frankie was banging on our front door. Frankie was so inconsiderate, she clearly forgot the fact that we now have a newborn in the house and that she, our ever so innocent and delicate little one, may be sleeping and not used to the whole Frankie drama and her over the top noise. However, the baby remained undisturbed. Frankie and her clamorous callous carriage didn't even provoke a stir in my precious dear granddaughter.

Frankie was furious and wild with rage. She barely took a breath whilst filling us in on all the details of the latest wayward White events. She excruciatingly kept repeating the same thing over and over.

'Them fucking cunning cunting gavers couldn't fucking wait to ruin my fucking Will J! They wanna do their fucking jobs properly and go catch some fucking nonces instead of running after my boy.' Frankie also said, 'They found fuck-all.'

But I saw them take all sorts with them, they put everything in those clear plastic zip bags, they even took a laptop and other Apple gadgets. The police probably had a field day in there as Frank and Will's boys had every latest gadget on the market. One good thing about technology is it can sometimes leave a very incriminating trail. Dodgy little shit Will J White was, let's hope they keep him locked up longer this time. Now he is one danger to society. Not that I said this out loud. Jesus I think Frankie would actually cut me. So messy, I genuinely don't know how she lives like it. Well I do, money. Frankie bought the baby a Juicy Couture tracksuit and a pair of pink Ugg boots. Sadie was made right up. Frankie broached the subject of naming the baby, something Sadie just couldn't seem to decide on. Frank was listing off all sorts.

'What about Tulula? Bronwyn? Aww Lacy, I like Lace for short! Then again Taylor is nice but really popular Sade! I know, Nora that's what I'd have Sade! Aww I don't know just there's so many lovely, nice girls' names out there! Patience is pretty too...'

Then Sadie just blurted it out, 'Kate, baby Kate, yes that's it, after you, Mum.' So that was it my granddaughter finally had a name. It only took a week! Bless my beautiful girls. Frankie brought baby Josh round too and when he was laid next to baby Kate he looked huge and she looked so tiny and fragile.

'They're gonna be best buddies and maybe even one day boyfriend and girlfriend,' squalled Frankie.

'Na I don't think so!' snapped Sadie with glaring eyes.

Frank gave a look, but I just rolled my eyes as if to say ignore her, she's hormonal. Luckily enough Frank didn't seem that bothered. I was cringing, but silently thought sometimes things are best ignored, certainly where Sadie is concerned. Frankie then only went and brought up the subject of baby Kate's dad. I couldn't believe it. Here Frank was standing in my kitchen inquisitively looking at baby Kate sleeping peacefully in her mosey basket, dressed head to toe in Armani looking absolutely fucking immaculate, as she always did. No matter how hectic and dysfunctional her life was you could guarantee Frank would be perfectly made up. Don't get me wrong not a bit of class about her and she is probably wearing over fifteen hundred pounds worth of clothes right now. That's without the fake tits, fake nails, fake lips, fake hair, and the fake tan. The list is endless.

I find it shocking how the Frankies of our society get away with claiming as single parents, they walk around dressed like wannabe wags, drive a top of the range oversized pollution buster, have more cosmetic surgery and procedures than the stars, enjoy fine five-star holidays, and then they even have the audacity to plaster this all over social media and more! Talk about rubbing it in your face! And yet still they feel the need to claim the poxy pennies us true single parents have to struggle to survive on. Yes these wannabe 'social wags' shall we call them, end up spending their so-called fair share of benefits on a pair of shoes a week whilst the likes of us 'do-gooders' scrub away with holes in our soles. It absolutely amazes me! She then goes on to say,

'Fuck's sake, Kate, you never gonna believe it I only got a letter from the old quacks this morning saying that they think John Boy needs reassessing! That was that old cunt of a nurse last time we had an appointment she told me straight that too many children are getting a diagnosis of ADHD when all is required is some good old fashioned discipline!'

'Oh shit, Frank, that's not good for you! What will you do?' I responded in an empathetic tone.

Through fits of laughter Frank replied, 'What I always do keep taking him back down the fucking doctors they soon refer me back I'm telling ya! I get so much on their case, like proper lay it on, I tell em I'm not sleeping I get some pills at least! Cheeky bastards they're a bunch of Indian givers, give it out in one hand mate then the rotten bastards take it back with the other!'

I simply say, 'Oh Frank you crack me up!' Like seriously William and Frankie live together, basically when he isn't shagging another piece of skirt William is always at home and even when he is getting his willy wet he always provides Frankie with more money a week than I earn in a month. Yet Frankie still manages to get more benefits than most. Every kid of hers has had or got or will have ADHD and consequently, or bizarrely should I say, our lovely democratic government feels the need to chuck an extra bundle of pounds every month at the crafty delinquent. And Frankie is not silly she knows she will get this for each naughty spawn that is born. Hence Frankie is already taking baby Josh to the doctors complaining that he doesn't sleep. And hey ho, good old doc gives Frank pills for him, not that she gives them to him, again she is not a silly girl, like why would she ever want to pump drugs into her own baby unless they were unwell, like really unwell, not just hyper or bored! But she is all too aware that this is a ticket as such to getting extra points towards a diagnosis of ADHD which will eventually ensure Frankie of her future extra benefit payments for baby Josh. I know, complex. But believe me,

I see and hear this shit all the time, it's happening right now! My question is who is to blame? The politicians? The doctors? The parents? Fuck knows! It goes on everywhere, the heroin addicts, the alcoholics and the crackheads, apparently all get more than the single parent. Get this, I even heard through the grapevine that the government give these unfortunates extra money for owning a dog! What an insult! May I add that this is all tax-free, national insurance-free, student loan-free, oh and yes pension-free. It's hilarious when compared to that of a genuine single parent who is commonly known to barely survive on one-fifth of what the Frankies of our society get, yet believe it or not yes some of those benefit busting single parents have been known to work their fingers to the bone and live for the thief who can get them knocked off food to survive.

As judgemental as it sounds the majority of ADHD diagnosed children are simply running the roost and need some good old fashioned discipline! Out of the mouth of the specialist nurse! No wonder single parents have earned such a stigma. However, I would be very intrigued to know who makes the decision to allow fatherless children to live in such poverty when in effect they too have been forced into a life of disadvantage and whilst at the same time think it acceptable to chuck a bundle of extras to those who misbehave, like that of the extra cash, discounts on travel, the gym, the theatre, the cinema and concert tickets are all included in the 'extra naughty bundle' shall we call it! Still to me it still doesn't make sense! What about the well-behaved ones or the conformists of our society? Where's their reward? My Sadie often asked why was it that the naughty children got took out on more school trips than the good children! I never had an answer to this other than it will pay off eventually to be good Sadie! The truth was I could never get my head around rewarding those who misbehave. Yet I would also sometimes wish Sadie was a bit naughty, as I might just get a little extra financial help. Terrible of me but when you see the extras, you can understand the reasons why people who exist on the breadline are inclined to bend the truth, if there's a chance to decrease the financial struggle you'd be a dense not to do it, certainly where I come from.

Forget honesty, just think it's a day out once a month, or the gas and electric, oh and shopping without adding up as you go around and having to embarrassingly put items back at the till as you have gone over and really don't have the £2.69 for the extra fruit you bought! See the thing is when you live on such a small budget a few hundred extra a month feels like you've won the lottery! It's sad as it's not even a huge amount but by golly it can make a huge difference.

One-parent families, whether it is mum or dad running the roost, I am 99% sure if you asked the majority of these people that currently live in the UK right now whether they would choose the deprived and underprivileged downtrodden life that seems to have befallen them, I don't think it would be a happy thanks or a high-five for Mr Tony

Blair or should I say Mr Cameron? Excuse my sarcasm. I would imagine that the single mothers of our society would rather have a happy husband who wants to protect and provide for his family and not leave it down to a distorted state to crush and scrutinise the mother's social failings. Anyway, again Frankie was the perfect example of a state abuser, she wouldn't even be able to comprehend my thoughts on her and her kind! However, in turn, people like Frank certainly didn't help the shit shame that true single mummas took the brunt of. Frankie, I would describe as thick not ignorant. But then I think about it and seriously I had to give the greedy leech some credit she had learnt the loops within the benefits system better than their very own stuck-up- your-own-arse judgemental job advisors and then used it to her own advantage. Clearly Frankie was far from a struggling silly single run-ragged mummy like the majority of us.

Then again looking at what was unfolding before my eyes, thick did often spring to my mind with Frankie, you think she would have clocked Sadie's temperamental mood about the father of her new baby, but obviously not. The stupid, insensitive, wannabe wag that she was couldn't possibly think about sensitivity. The thoughtless cow only blurted out,

'So why you not letting on who her father is then, Sade? Frank is still cooing away at the baby, absolutely oblivious to Sadie glaring wide-eyed up at her from the chair over by the breakfast bar. Then off the silly cow went again, Frank didn't realise what her wayward mouth was getting her into. 'Well Sadie, baby Kate is gonna need er daddy, he's got rights too ya know!' Frankie's words were said loud and clear. I didn't even get a chance to say anything and from out of nowhere Sadie was dragging Frank out of the house screaming.

'He'll never have rights, cause he'll never fucking know, so keep your fucking big cunt nose out.' Sadie slammed the door. Now Frank was going crazy at the door, baby Kate was screaming, Sadie was crying cradling the baby in an attempt to try and calm her. Josh, clearly a familiar milieu for the dear boy, had slept through the whole ordeal. I took him straight out to Frank and apologised for Sadie. Frank seemed to care more about her clothes and her hair extensions and whether or not they were damaged rather than Sadie totally losing the plot on her. Frank was so superficial even I was shocked. She even shouted back,

'Tell Sade don't feel bad, I was thirteen once.'

Frank did baffle me; I never really knew what she meant. Don't feel bad for having sex? Bad for getting pregnant? Bad for attacking her? Bad for not telling anyone who the father is? Who knows, but at least she didn't want to fall out. I could do without the drama.

Even though I thought Sadie was bang out of order I would still defend her, no matter what, and if she's not ready to tell anyone who the father is then that's fine but fuck I must stress to her that she can't attack people when they ask about him.

# Four

It was the hottest day of the year so far, it was my first day off from work for weeks and I was making the most of the rays, laying on a sun lounger in the garden drinking a glass of vodka and cranberry; it should feel like heaven for me right now.

As much as I was trying hard to switch off I still felt agitated. The last few months had been a fucking crazy rollercoaster of a journey. Sadie and baby Kate were at my mum's for the weekend. So here I was absolutely free. I felt a bit bored if I were honest and I find it insane how we mums crave a break and then when we very rarely get that ever so needed space that we yearn for, we feel completely and utterly lost. I guess this is just another lonely factor of being an unloved single mummy. It makes me think of the new common saying I hear of late; M.I.L.F 'Mum I'd like to fuck'! Says it all really about the society we are living in and how the male species of the twenty-first century perceive mummies!

I'm not back at work until Monday morning and the girls are not back until Monday night. In all fairness I have not had a break since baby Kate was born and should be relishing this time. If I've not been running around after

Sadie and the baby, I've been flat out cleaning for all and sundry, although the money comes in handy, I constantly feel exploited, it helps but still I feel like I am drowning in my bills most of the time. To top it off Sadie has been a complete nightmare the last few months, not going to school, drinking, back chatting me and basically just being an arsehole, which is a joke when I'm the one running around sorting childcare out for the baby and then she doesn't even bother turning up at school. Her drinking is getting out of control and she's staying out until all hours, I just don't know what to do. So I thought a weekend with Nanny Anna might help. My mother certainly won't tolerate any of Sadie's bullshit. My mother is what you would call a woman of God. She was once, shall we say, a foolish woman and now she has found faith. I'm sure Sadie will be impressed with my mother's Godly friends. I laugh at this thought and think, have that, Sadie bloody Andrews!

I'm glad my mum doesn't live around the corner anymore, certainly at times like this. Sidcup I think is far away enough from here for Sadie not to venture back home to see her mates and get herself into trouble. It wasn't all bad though, I received my acceptance into college this week and so did a few friends so we are all going for celebratory drinks this evening. I really don't know what the fuck I'm going to wear. It's not like I have an abundance of clothes and certainly don't have the pennies for anything new. I haven't been out in months. Actually I think it was well before Christmas, it's probably closer to a year. When I think about this I get quite anxious at the thought of venturing out on the tiles. I should try not to leave it so long and then maybe I wouldn't feel so nervous. I couldn't explain these nerves it just happens when I go out into the night. I think it must be an age thing or maybe it's my own inadequate feeling about my situation! Sometimes I think we crazy creatures crave love but when it comes down to it our own failings or misfortune prevent us fulfilling that and that's why I get these anxious feelings, when I put myself into the potential dating zone. Gosh I am such a deep thinker.

I might ask Frank to borrow something to wear although she is much bustier than me, albeit false, she is the same size as me everywhere else, she has some beautiful clothes and they are all designer. I text Frank and within half an hour she is round at mine with what looks like her entire wardrobe. Frankie is hilariously cunning, she told Will that I'm having a mental breakdown and really needed cheering up so he must look after the kids. How he took that I'll never know. But she did say he was licking her arse at the minute because she found some old mort's long copper hair in his trousers. Frank's blonde, bright bleached blonde. She just brushes it off and makes the most out of the fact she caught him out and that he will be the perfect partner for a week or so. Crazy relationship but somehow it works. Under all the clothes were a few handbags, out of one Frank pulled a bottle of Pink Moet. Frank loved a glass of champers, she wasn't really into Lambrini.

William told Frankie he would take the kids to his mother's for a couple of hours so therefore Frankie took full advantage of Will's absence and insisted that, 'we both need to get sorted and get out before the old bastard gets back!'

Now Frank's decided she's coming out I will be on tenterhooks waiting for William White to show up and kick off. But how could I say no, I am borrowing her; red skinny Armani Jeans, her black Jimmy Choo stilettos, a black lace, brand new may I add, Gucci top, an amazing Mulberry bag, and some beautiful dress jewellery apparently from some shop in Blue Water. Although I feel a million dollars the evening looks as if it will be a disaster. Frank disappearing like she has, means William will only hunt her down or have one of his cronies stake us out, so there will definitely be no chance of pulling any talent. This was not one of the bonuses of living next door to Frank and William White.

We were just finishing our drinks in the Tavern and as I expected it had been a bit of a wash out of an evening. I spent most the night looking for Frankie. She spent more time in the toilets sniffed out of her nut than anywhere else, she has drunk more than most of the men in here but still she stands, albeit half-dressed, she has even managed to lose her Dior jacket and is also somehow missing a very expensive Christian Louboutin shoe. How? I do not know. As shocked as I am at least there was no William White drama. We got a taxi pretty easy considering the state Frankie was in. I was dreading the fact I was going to have to physically take Frank to her door, she was in no fit state to walk on her own. What on earth was William going to say? However, to my surprise, before we even got out of the cab Will was there paying the driver. I felt utter relief as I would have used the last of my money and I don't get paid until Monday. What a nightmare, thank God the girls are away this weekend. At least I won't have to worry about shopping. William was pleasant enough. He certainly is licking arse. How bizarre he didn't even ask where Frankie's missing shoe and jacket were. I think he would have definitely noticed as he was holding her like you would hold a baby and at the same time covering up her half-dressed body with his own dressing gown. Funny that I never imagined William White to be the dressing gown type.

I was sitting at the kitchen table mulling over the events of the evening, thinking fuck, how am I so fucking goddamn lonely? The loneliness wraps itself around you like a big dark heavy blanket. It actually hurts, physically hurts. The tears spring to my eyes and they flow once again without warning. I consider myself to be an attractive woman, no supermodel but I scrub up well enough to turn heads. To be honest plenty of cocks admire me; bit too skinny but great arse I'd often get told! Fuckable eyes apparently! Really since when do we fuck in the eye? I have mousy blonde shoulder-length hair that always frizzes up when wet. Personally I hate my frizzy hair, however, again many cocks have complimented me on my hair being real! We do live in a time of fakery so I guess it's rare to find a natural.

I think that's another problem in our society today, fake and false as fuck! No wonder we lonely orgasms have lost faith! And yet as fuckable as I'm supposed to be, I'm still sat here again on my fucking Jonas. I guess this singleness is through choice as clearly I could get a fuck but at what worthless cost?

I'd like to say its society's fault for producing a bunch of womanising sniff heads who don't give a fuck about love, loyalty, trust, sexual connection, sustainability, their offspring etc. However when I really analyse this generation I've been born into, can society really take the blame? Surely it has something to do with what we, us women allow or even nurture!

Nonetheless, I can say one hundred percent I am not willing to accept the faulty fruits that are on offer today but where does that leave me and the rest of the mes of our society? Undesired and unlovable or temporarily fuckable? Shutting down to this, you in turn become a lonely orgasm. That's what my friends and myself describe ourselves as. We laugh when this is said but we all know it's actually far from funny. I think it's fucking sad to be honest.

The lost generation mate. That's what I say.

# Five

BANG BANG BANG... Fuck! Who the fuck could that be at this time of night? Please not Fiona, not again!

'Kate it's me, Will, open up now, I need to talk to you!' The manly tone sounded wild and I instantly knew it was William White that was banging my door down and now he was peering through my letter box.

'Hold on a minute I need to get my keys,' I sheepishly shout out to William.

His eyes were now fixated on my crotch area, the irony, I thought, was hilarious. Two knowingly big brown eyes leering away at my un-loveable box. I am rummaging through Frankie's tiny Mulberry bag that I had borrowed earlier, to find my keys. Why are they always so hard to find? Found them! Duh they're not in the bag! Why did he, William White, always make me so goddamn flustered? I say this under my breath. I'm definitely that person that speaks to herself in silence a lot. There they were! Sitting right in front of me on the rocking chair at the bottom of the stairs next to the front door, the ever so overgrown bundle of imitation silver and gold that I had acquired were glistening away at me. Looking so rich and full. Mocking really, considering they are effectively my bread and butter. I didn't even get a chance to open the door wide enough for myself to even see the man before me and in barged William straight past me into the kitchen as if he owned the place.

'Fuck's sake, Kate, what's been going on tonight? Her fucking phone keeps going off and I am not best pleased at what I'm fucking reading! Who the fuck is Barney, Kate?'

His face was wild with rage. Contorted. His top lip slightly curled up in the right corner. I think his bottom lip was actually trembling. Still I felt a pang of sadness for this big burly handsome brute standing so refined in my kitchen.

'Whoa hold on Will, I ain't got a clue what you're ranting on about,' I responded very honestly. But in all fairness I genuinely did not know what William was going on about. Maybe it was the coke. Maybe Frank's dealer has been messaging her. Fucked if I knew. William was wild, I actually thought he was going to launch himself at me. But instead he flung Frank's phone at me. I caught it. Well done me. I am normally absolutely shockingly crap at catch. I automatically read.

Barney: You dirty fucking whore I love it when you just show up and surprise me x

Frank: I be up for seconds in a minute. Just sending dozy bollox to the bar. She be half hour. The queue from here back to the Bull.

Frank: Where are you big bollox?

Frank: ffs I need your big hard cock inside my tight pussy xxxx

Barney: 2 min stuck. And I want to be stuck in you. I'm cummmmmiiinnnggg hahaha
Barney: You love it hard and deep still then I see
Barney: You coming for thirds you dirty whore
Barney: Frank party at mine. You & me and loads of coca & cocka hahaha

I slowly look up at William. 'Oh shit, I actually don't know what to say, I'm so shocked, Will.' I think my voice told him I was as shocked as he was. Although I could see the man was pissed off, and he had every right to be yet I still couldn't help feel a pang of embarrassment at how Frankie described me as a 'dozy bollox'! The fucking cheek of it!

Will was now a little calmer. This hard strong man sitting at my makeshift breakfast bar looked forlorn. I think he actually had tears in his eyes. I offered him a drink. I did not know what else to do. The only thing I had was vodka. I poured myself one, I think I needed it. At any minute I expected him to go into a mad crazy rage. However, he seemed gutted. Again, another emotion I have never seen in William White's eyes. The only time I have ever seen him looking gutted is when the boys in blue arrest him.

He looked at me and said, 'Why? Why Kate? I give the fucking girl everything. Alright I've had me fair share of flings but fuck she knows what it is and I always come back home to her and my boys.'

All sorts of thoughts were running through my head. I was speechless - which is so unlike me. I poured us another vodka. This carried on until 3am, well that was the last time I looked at the clock, before I became too drunk. I woke at 6am, naked. Fuck. Oh fuck. Will is lying next to me. Oh fuck, fuck, fuck. What do I do? I freeze. He is sparko. Flashes of last night's events were anxiously flickering into my conscious. Visions of me riding William and him grabbing at my arse pulling and pushing himself deeper into me. And still his half-naked toned torso is on display arousing my innermost yearnings. He hasn't changed a bit really from all those years ago. The same strong tanned muscular ripped physique, quite perfect really. William White was one seriously hot man.

Fuck! Fuck! I have done it again. Oh god Kate, you and your deprived vagina and vodka and a no-go man is not a good concoction. Fuck that it's your mate's partner and the fucking biggest supplier of drugs and god knows what else in the Medway towns. Oh yeah and the other teeny tiny slight little problem you have is that he is the so-called dead father of your fucking daughter! Gosh what would he do if he ever found out? His only daughter and it's all my own doing, it's me who has hid her for all these years effectively depriving him of his only daughter. I think he would hate me forever. Sadie would definitely hate me. I hate me.

Shit he's stirring. Oh fuck his hands are wandering. He has his hand on my sex-crazed delicate illicit little box. Fuck what do I do? Oh shit he is groaning, excitedly. Oh no, now he is rubbing his very own excited morning glory up the side of my thigh. I am so tense he must know I am not sleeping. However my vagina is throbbing insatiably. Oh no a finger is slipping in. Talk about is this how they wake up every fucking morning? Couples that is. Well my body seems to be responding in a way that I can't seem to control. I am wild for him. Fuck! William then whispers in my ear.

'Kate I want you, fuck how did I ever forget about you?' I stayed silent. But just allowed my body to respond naturally and enjoy the tender touches and the deepness that fulfilled my innermost desires. So selfish of me. But clearly my body is clashing with my mind. My body succumbs. I orgasm several times. Shit why did William White do this to me. I detest the man. I am shocked at how he's wrapped himself around me and that he seems very content laying in our tranquil love juices.

I break the silence and say, 'I think you should probably go next door before the neighbours, or even worse, Frank rises.'

He flatly responded, 'Fuck Frank, Kate, and seriously, Kate, I think the neighbours have seen a whole lot worse. Don't you?'

I tried to get out of his grip. 'I need a shower,' I say desperately.

William begrudgingly released me and replied seductively, 'Only on the condition I get to watch you bend over and wash your toes Miss Andrews.' I couldn't help but laugh. He was so crude. But fuck he turned me on. It was like he could manipulate and control my body not just with his hands and his hardness but also with his way of words. I yield to his being. For me this is a dangerous point. Feelings erupt. This I know from experience always ends up hurting. The pathetic princess dream that most of us women desire is bullshit. The euphoria is soon met with disillusionment. The unexpected sensational high a lover can give you is insane in comparison to that of the predictable expected disappointment they always seem to deliver with perfection. It's like the male species have mastered rejection and are still in primary education when it comes to loving one woman for longer than a month. Basically I know what is to come. The wild night of passion is soon to be met with pure ignorance. The bullshit talk. But I still say to myself or should I say my unconscious grumbles away at my consciousness, 'You never know Kate he could be the one.' This I say is hope in the finest form. Hope for that fairy tale. Whatever the consequence in some cases.

Well the shower experience certainly was one I won't forget. The water cascading our nakedness, the heat, the bare skin, our hands carelessly caressing and douching each other. Will's hands are so strong and god I felt them, certainly when he pulled at my hair whilst I was on my knees sucking his somewhat very large hard cock. I love a cheeky clean cock! William undeniably relished a woman on her knees. The water was drenching our bodies almost into a state of catharsis. God, I can still smell him. A mix of his and my own love juices entwined with his Jean Paul

Gaultier aftershave that still bitterly lingered on my unwashed sheets.

Masturbation will never be able to satisfy the bittersweet desires that one can only achieve through hot, hard, horny sex. I knew this but still it didn't mean that I really wanted to admit this fact. It's pretty much like saying 'I need a man' and that I do not ever want to have to admit to, or even succumb to. Kate you're a fucking walking contradiction, even if I say so myself.

Well that was nearly 24 hours ago. I have not heard a dickie bird from either Frankie or William. I am still laying in my very sexed-up bed. Too scared to venture down. What has he told Frankie? If he has? What about Barney? Oh god! What will become of me? I am an absolute crap awful whore of a friend!

Jesus it's only five past six. Sadie and baby Kate are not home until tomorrow evening. I can't stay here any longer laying in my dirty deceitful laundry it's almost like waiting for my treacherous debauchery to be exposed through that of my filthy two-faced sheets. I will call Laney, yes that's what I will do. I need someone to offload too, someone not too close but close enough.

# Six

I had known Laney May Meeks since secondary school. Laney was a good girl, from a lovely area in Rochester, St Margaret Street. God what an address.

It was a big house, detached, with dormer windows on the first floor, double garage and a jacuzzi, you know not the kind of house you find in the middle of a council estate. I will always remember her floor tiles in the ever so spacious hall. I now know that they most definitely were the original tiles from the Victorians, probably restored, obviously by a specialist. They were beautiful, a black and white bold design with a flash of orange. Something I had only seen in the museum in Rochester. Dickens eat your heart out style.

It's funny the things you remember. Like really what thirteen-year-old girl takes such an interest in a friend's floor tiles. Most of them were popping pills and giving blow jobs out like they were gobstoppers. I, however, was more interested in people and how people lived, unbelievable at thirteen but true. Therefore to say the obvious, Laney May Meeks didn't end up pregnant at an unripe age or a ripe age for the fact. Neither did she find herself destined to live in a council house at any age let alone at the fresh age of sixteen. She moved to Spain ten years ago but has been back home a couple of years now. Laney lives out by Sevenoaks on a farm that she inherited from a great uncle. Laney never had kids and never married. She inherited a lot of money from just about every uncle and aunt and long lost relative she ever had. Consequently Laney is, shall we say, enjoying life to the absolute max.

Imagine not worrying about a bill or making sure your money stretches the week just so you can cover food, electric and gas. In all fairness we can scrimp on the gas, we can deal with wearing extra clothes but we cannot deal with no light and a rumbling tummy. Oh to live the other way. The Laney way, six-plus holidays a year and a five-star luxury lifestyle with no fucking bills at the end. Yes I would say Laney May Meeks was one lucky lady.

She was thrilled when I phoned her and asked if I could come and verbally abuse her. She responded excitedly with 'I am already doing brunch for us both. As we speak. Right now. So I suggest you get your tight little arse over here Miss Andrews! Right now!' Laney didn't shock me with her flirtatious way. Laney was always so blunt but because she spoke very well, rather posh to be true, really I think that's why she seemed to get away with some of her strange and even inappropriate innuendos. To be honest, I've always thought that Miss Meeks desires both sexes. There were a few rumours floating around at school and as we all know there is never smoke without fire. Well Laney was as pissed as a fart by the time I arrived, which may I add was ten past ten on a Sunday morning. She looked a complete mess. I had never seen her so bedraggled.

Laney was quite eccentric with her style. Wispy and floaty. Colourful clothes. A proper sixties stoner look. Well this morning she was going for the scary Mary look. Leggings that were so tight her camel toe looked more like a pregnant camel toe which she had carelessly matched with a psychedelic tight fitting belly top. Laney certainly has a great pair of tits and a good, rounded figure. As you can imagine this look does not do her any justice certainly when she is wearing size four clothes and she's clearly a curvaceous size twelve. I think she forgets we are no longer sweet sixteen. Maybe that's what not having children does to you. You squeeze into thirteen-year-old's clothes. It's like me wearing Sadie's clothes. I giggle at the thought.

Sadie lives in tracksuit and trainers. A complete tomboy is my Sade. Total opposite of myself. I would describe myself as a skinny jeans and leather jacket kinda girl, denim shorts and a vest in the summer, and a good old faithful black dress for special occasions and in the mean time I choose to save the tracksuit and trainers look for my teenager. Laney insisted we have prosecco with our lunch. Not that she needed anymore. I did try saying I was actually really hungover because of my recent shenanigans. However, Laney was clearly on another planet. Every time I tried to say about William, Laney would fall asleep. Although she stayed seated at the table and managed to keep hold of her wine glass she had her eyes shut and her head down throughout lunch.

I think I could have told her I fucked Tony Blair whilst Cherie was watching and she still wouldn't have raised an eyebrow. Seriously, I don't know what's going on with Laney but hell she's not quite here with me right now. So to my utter annoyance, I have still not spoke a word about last night and about William fucking White. Oh fuck. What will become of me?

Anyway, enough of me. I am such a self-absorbed selfish awful friend. Laney what the fuck are you doing? I could not believe my eyes. She has now gone from pretty much falling asleep whilst eating lunch to some crazy, half-naked creature dancing erotically. Her bare body cavorting all over the kitchen sides, up and down the fridge she gyrates and up and down the freezer she frolics. All the while a really loud Janis Joplin's 'Cry Baby' blares from her integrated sound system. I couldn't turn it down if I tried, let alone turn it off. Wow she was far too close for comfort. She was now topless. Yes pert, no- baby titties for Laney, and her very large erect nipples are now eyeballing me, she is actually now rotating her body around my own body. I freeze. She slowly wriggles herself away onto the large leather black sofa that sat lost in her huge kitchen and then to my absolute shock she slid her free hand, yes the one not holding her glass goes into her leggings and yes, wow, Laney is blatantly masturbating right in front of my own eyes. Again I freeze, for what feels like hours, however, it must have only been at least a minute or two and then I scream at her.

'What the fuck, Lane?'

It was like she was in some sort of trance. She snapped herself straight up, immediately removed her free hand from her pants, and looked straight at me and said.

'So sorry babe, what with the pills, the alcohol, and you, I just lose myself and forget that we are both floating on different spectrums at this present time in our lives.' Although clearly Laney was giving me some narcotic-fuelled philosophical speech about life, existence, sexuality, and love, however, I would never in a million years expect what was to come next.

So eventually after me listening and nodding to a load of fucking bull-shit, Laney declared her undying love for me. Yes can you believe this?! Apparently this is why she moved two thousand miles away all those years ago. She couldn't bear to see me or be around me. Apparently it was too hard for her not to be able to touch me or kiss me. I could not believe my ears. Where the fuck did all this come from? How do I even get myself out of this? I was stunned and speechless. Laney was pouring me a tequila shot now. Oh god as much as I needed it, I can't. It was essential I keep a straight head. I ignore her gesture for the shot and put the kettle on. I need a coffee and in my nice diplomatic tone suggest she have one with me and that way we can talk soberly. I don't think she was too keen, but somehow I saw a little light of hope in her eyes and she said,

'Of course, Kate, whatever will make you happy and if it is coffee that will make you take me seriously then coffee we will have.' Well with that she starts off on another rant about how could I not feel this heat between us? And how she thinks I'm in denial. Jesus knock me over again. There seems to be no way out for me. I apologise that I never knew that she felt this way. But fuck I am not a lesbian. I have never been a big fan of rug munching myself, but everyone to their own. I try to say this to Laney again in a diplomatic way. Obviously no rug munching talk or minge-eater talk. I actually explain that it's cock I crave and not crack. However, she thinks I'm taking the piss and I'm really not. Then this sends her off into some fury and provokes the man-hater inside her. I need to escape rapidly.

'I hate men too,' I say and realise very quickly that this is not the best thing to say to a lesbian who is declaring her undying love to you and believes that you are in denial. I then quickly re-phrase my 'I hate men' to 'I have to love to hate men.' She did look rather confused. At that point I noticed she was swigging the tequila from the bottle also with her free hand in her pants again. This time sitting on the stool at the breakfast bar. Clearly no shame. Again, maybe this is what not having kids does to you. No more lonely orgasms. Do a Laney, find an audience! To my absolute relief within seconds she is asleep. Still holding the tequila and still she has her free hand down her pants. Head flat down on her cold diamond-encrusted granite worktop. I do not hesitate my immediate escape. I cannot wonder and wait. I am in the car and at least 30 seconds go by before I let myself think about what I may be going home to. Surely it can't be as bad as what I'm running from now?

## Seven

All was quiet. No Frankie and no William White. I felt nervous. I do not know whether this uneasy feeling was because of Frankie or William; either way the whole situation provoked the anxiety within me more than ever before. The house was eerily quiet. No Sadie. No baby Kate. No elephant running up and down the stairs. That's how I described Sadie. She was so loud my girl. Never discreet and quiet. Even when she sleeps she snores like a grizzly bear. It's unbearable. But I miss my elephant bear and her very own baby bear, as demanding as they are, babies, that is. Well to be honest compared to Sadie as a baby, baby Kate is a walk in the park. I couldn't leave the room without Sadie going psycho baby crazy on me. However baby Kate is so content, as long as she got her muslin, she's like a pig in shit, as my nan would say. Can't say I like that saying, certainly now that I have wrote it to say aloud! Baby Kate is like a princess in love. Oh I do have to laugh at my own connotations.

I was in the garden watering my very thirsty plants. What with all the shenanigans the last couple of days, my dear plants have been neglected. Extra feed this evening.

Fiona shouted over the fence, 'Is that you babe?'

I replied sheepishly, 'Yes lovely lady, how are you?' I see her hands at the top of the fence panel, I can imagine her climbing onto her bench so she can see me.

'All good my babe! Fucking hell you missed the biggest of showdowns, literally half hour ago. Frank begging Will not to leave her, yes he was leaving not being chucked out.' All wide-eyed was Fi and very inquisitive as she chats away in her very dramatic manner. I think, take a breath Fiona. 'Frank was on the floor begging, arms wrapped around his legs, cor Kate what a drama, thought I was on the set of EastEnders,' Fiona sarcastically said with a grin and a deep breath.

I tried to appear as casual as ever. 'Fuck knows, Fi. I'm sure they're both be fine, Fi, you know them two.' I think I say this convincingly. And off our Fi-Fi goes again. I smile at her enthusiasm.

'Well he fucked off in his big truck thing and I see her packing her motor up with the kids. I did go out there but she was too upset to make any sense out of her. She did say though, Kate, to ask me to get you to call her.' I think my face showed the dread I felt, as before I even had a chance to respond Fiona was laughing hysterically saying. 'Well you are Dear Deidre of the street of course she gonna wanna bore your ears off with another one of their dysfunctional family fucking dramas.' Fiona was such a piss taker, albeit in a nice way. I replied sensitively,

'Oh stop it Fi, I'll give her a bell in a bit.' But literally as I said that my phone started buzzing away. I look at Fi and mouth 'It's Frank.' Like Frank can hear me! Why do we whisper like this when we don't really want to answer the call to someone in particular? Like they can hear us! Perhaps it's the guilt!

Fi shouts, 'Answer it then you silly cow.' Shit just for a moment I think I let my saucy shame slip but Fi shows no signs of seeing my real reasons behind not wanting to take Frank's call.

I simply press the green button and cringingly say, 'Hello Frank.' With that I hear a sobbing Frank at the other end. It literally sounds like she is calling from the middle of the South Pacific. I can barely hear her. Although I do hear snot, lots of snot being sniffed. Well at least I think it's snot and not cocaine. Eventually I make out the words she mumbles. I reply flatly, 'No babe I haven't seen him.' Apparently he has left her. Moved out for good this time. Frank is a mess and in no fit state to talk. To the point her mum eventually took the phone from Frank and shouted,

'The dinny cunt's done it this time ain't she, fucking silly shrivelling div that she is.' And with that Frank's mum, Maureen, laughs a catty laugh down the phone and continued with her verbal mishandling of the situation. 'I told her to stop fucking playing around, it always comes out in the fucking wash, silly cunt, she can't even talk. I'll get her to call you back Kate when she sorted herself out, the pathetic twat. Tulla.' And the phone went dead.

Frank's mum was the same as Frank they both had never possessed a polite telephone manner. Fiona loved a bit of a gossip and couldn't wait to indulge in this. I wasn't giving anything away. Who the fuck was I to judge, considering my latest salaciousness? Fuck, I needed a drink. Nothing absolutely nothing in. Not a drop in sight. Oh hang on I found a little can of vodka and cranberry. That must be Sadie's as I never put alcohol in the cereal cupboard. Just what I need. I'm not moaning. I pour it into a glass of ice and quickly drain. I so enjoyed that. I want another one. Problem is I'm going to have to walk to the shop which means I could get tied up with Fiona and her questions about Frank and William. My desire for alcohol wins and I chance the Fi-Fi interrogation.

With my last ten pounds I skip my way to the shop. That will get me a few more cans. Surely. I don't actually know how much these things cost. I don't normally drink alcohol its only on special occasions I indulge. I feel rather fluffy. It's amazing what alcohol does to me. Even just the one. I like this feeling right now. Oh and check me out, I'm clearly letting off the pheromones as well. The poor window cleaner has just fallen off the ladder to get a look at oneself. I feel rather embarrassed to be honest. Poor thing. Not that I am going over to lick his wounds. I felt like I was hot stuff. What with the sex. The lesbian act. The alcohol and now the poor window cleaner's misfortunate fall. A hot and horny Kate was on the loose. This could be dangerous. However I have my mojo back. It's been a long time coming. And fuck, to my utter fucking hazy surprise, as I come out of the shop, he is there. Right in front of me.

Standing bold as you like in my path. Yes the fucking irritatingly hot Mr fucking White. Grinning his big white smile at me. Little old Kate. Yes me. Little old fucking Katie Andrews.

'Looking fuckable as per usual,' he whispers into my ear. I smile and walk on. All the while thinking, yippee I look fuckable! And wow back at ya! Have you looked in the mirror recently Will! And shit he is now shouting my name out in broad daylight and open air fucking public.

'Kate! Kate!' I never realised how much I loved hearing him, his voice say my name.

I swing around and stroppy me shouts, 'Not now Will! And aint you going in the shop?'

He is so fucking goddamn trim. He oozes testosterone. Dark hair. Dark Eyes. At least six foot two. A body most men work hard for. But not for William White. God was certainly feeling exceptionally generous when dishing out the finer looks to Mr White. A naturally good-looking specimen. It doesn't help that he dresses impeccably either. Mont Clair. Rolex. Splash of Armani. Oh yeah and let's not forget the array of expensive motors he owns. He has his Range, some big truck thing, a sporty Audi, oh yeah and his beloved Frank's Golf convertible. Not that I'm great with cars but I must say he was in his Audi this eve and what a sexy little black number that one was.

So anyway he somehow manages to persuade me to get a lift with him, although I was insisting it's only a few minutes up the road and I'm more than capable of walking it. However, Mr White can be extremely persistent. Therefore he got his own way. However William White has another agenda and once again he has me in his grip. He wants to talk. Like really what the fuck is there to talk about? We fucked. End of. It can never happen again. There is just too much against this kind of catharsis. The carnage would be irreparable. Not that William White took me seriously in the slightest. Like I said, persistent is Mr White.

We were now driving towards the Robin Hood pub. A very old quaint English country pub. William very blatantly tells me we are going for a drink. He is so stern and completely dismissive of my spoken wants. However this only turns me on more. Then he proceeds to slowly touch my inner thigh. His manly hands caressing me. His finger couldn't resist. I feel myself take a breath, a deep breath as he entered me. I am so wet. I know this but William also excitedly points this fact out too.

'Mmm, you're soaking!' he growls seductively.

'Of course I am my nuni is slightly overwhelmed with all the attention. Here we are driving. Well you are driving and at the same time you are still managing to control my sexual wants and desires. Nunis, my darling, like cocks, can't hide their pleasure! Who said men can't multi task?'
I speak although I was clearly in another realm. I am throbbing insatiably for this man. I cannot resist to join William in touching oneself. It is orgasmic. Bob Marley's 'Homely Girl' blaring away in the background. The cars

speeding past as we join the dual carriageway to access the Robin Hood pub only heightened the drug-like feeling that I was experiencing.

William with his one finger still inside me. Me playing with my clitoris and also when William needed his free hand to change gear my own fingers couldn't help but react to my bodily wants, enough to make myself cum. Luckily I was wearing my tight little red dress which easily slid up enough to show my red lacy knickers and allow easy access to my little unloved box. I thought it only polite for him to taste. He seemed to enjoy. Yes one tanned leg was slightly slanted towards my man, my other tanned leg up on the dash, one of my high heels loosely hang on my right foot, my nuni on display for Will's eyes only, the feeling was euphoric looking at Will exploring my yearnings and enjoying me only heightened my ecstasy-like state. The black leather seats added to the sexual setting that was unfolding. After my own naughty orgasm I couldn't resist tasting Will. He was rock hard and in need. We pulled over in the country lane for that one. And god I could taste him all day long. William White certainly tasted like Tesco's finest selection. God that man must eat well.

# Eight

Sadie loved her baby, however, at times she felt like launching the screaming little mare out of the window. Having a baby can be said to be one of the most consuming and demanding things any parent can get themselves into. For Sadie this was a complete shock to the system. It was early evening on Saturday and Sadie had to endure the company of her nan for another night.

'I'm so bored,' moaned Sadie as she was folding washing from the line.

'You should make the most of the baby sleeping, go and have a nap with her, Sadie,' snapped her nan.

'Don't want sleep, thanks Nan. I just wanna get the fuck out of here! It's like a fucking morgue.' Sadie was harsh with her words.

'You cheeky little mare, all what me and your mother do for you, ungrateful little madam!' Sadie's nan was not best pleased with Sadie's attitude and continued to shout out all the things she and Sadie's mother have sacrificed for Sadie and baby Kate.

This did not go down too well with Sadie. Sadie stuck her middle finger up at her nan and screamed back at her, 'Fuck you all and fuck all you do for me.' With that Sadie stormed out the back door and by the sounds of it the back door was firmly shut. Why do we do that, slam a door in temper? Does this really make us feel better? But jeez, when I was younger it was a common occurrence to slam my bedroom door. I actually took the hinges off once.

Sadie ended up at the local park. She aimlessly wondered around realising she had come out with nothing, no phone, no purse, absolutely nothing. She could see a group of teenagers sitting over by the community centre. They were drinking and smoking what seem to smell suspiciously like cannabis. As Sadie walked by one of the lads shouted out at her.

'You alright?' He was the tallest of the group and appeared to be the cocky one. Sadie looked on and tried to avoid any engagement. However, the boy pursued Sadie. His name was Jack Mize he lived in Sidcup and he had lived there all his life. He told Sadie he was sixteen and looking for a girlfriend and that Sadie would be perfect for this position. Jack had a charming demeanour. The attention from Jack had made Sadie feel something, something other than anger, perhaps enjoyment. Sadie had been so numb since falling pregnant with baby Kate and now she felt a little warmth. Sadie was not in any rush to tell the group she was a mum. The shame and embarrassment that Sadie felt from becoming such a young mum had made Sadie look at herself very differently. Jack had made Sadie giggle that evening, something Sadie had been blind to for so long. Jack was a handsome young man, mousy brown hair, big blue eyes, and with a boxer's physique. Although Jack said he was a boxer, he also said he hasn't boxed for the last year because of an injury to his foot. He was run over by his own father. Jack said it was an accident.

There were around six or seven teenagers in the group but for Sadie it actually only felt like it was just Jack and Sadie. That was the first time Sadie had tried cannabis, she had experimented lots lately with alcohol and god that had got her in some seriously awkward situations. Like the time when she and her friend Tasha Nolan bunked off school and stole Tasha's mum's vodka and then went and got super drunk up the Jacksons. The Jacksons as it was called was a play park and a recreational field in Rochester. Then they both ended up getting arrested for stealing a pair of shoes from Primark in Chatham High Street. Then there was the time when Sadie stole the alcohol from Fiona next door. It was actually only a couple of weeks after baby Kate was born and Sadie had been feeling really angry over her mum not letting her go to The Casino Rooms. The Casino is a very popular nightclub in Rochester High Street. However they hold function nights for the under 18s. So Sadie thought it fit to steal Fiona's half-full bottle of gin. To say the least Sadie was in a complete state. Fiona found her out the back garages slumped over and covered in her own vomit. It took Fiona to pick her up and chuck her over her shoulder in order to get her round to her mother's. Kate and Fiona were both really worried because Sadie was unresponsive even after Kate threw water in her face. Kate eventually called an ambulance. The ambulance crew decided that they had to take Sadie to the hospital where they kept her in until the following day. Just to be safe, apparently. Therefore, poor Kate had to call her mum, get her down from Sidcup at silly o'clock to look after baby Kate whilst she herself stayed with her drunken daughter at the hospital. Sadie ended up being grounded for a whole month. But tonight was different, Sadie felt calm and hazy. Completely relaxed. Certainly not in the mood for any more dramas with her nan.

Jack insisted on walking Sadie all the way to the garden gate of her nan's house. Jack seemed so caring and polite. Although Sadie was sure both her nan and her mum would not like the fact he smoked weed. Jack would be deemed a druggy by the judgemental ignorance of her dear elders. Sadie felt her nan and mum were both so dramatic. They literally would class someone who smokes a bit of cannabis as a heroin addict. Sadie hoped her nan would not smell the cannabis. That's the last thing she needed right now. Sadie just wanted her bed and some sleep before baby Kate wakes her for another feed. To Sadie's surprise her nan didn't mention last night's events or even ask where Sadie had disappeared to. Sadie's nan was up at the crack of dawn and even sent Sadie back to bed for a couple of hours and took baby Kate out for a long walk. So when Sadie finally rose it was gone eleven. The sun was strikingly bright and appeared to be peering at Sadie through the pale lilac curtains that hung at the tiny window of her nan's spare room. The sun was shining directly on Sadie's face making her feel all safe and alive inside. Sadie was feeling so calm and chilled. This was so unusual for Sadie as she always felt rushed, stressed and angry at everything. However today, Sadie felt a little excited. I think Jack would certainly have something to do with Sadie's change of mood.

Sadie woke to several messages from Jack asking when they can meet up again and telling her how much he had enjoyed spending time with her last night. Sadie asked her nan.

'Would you mind watching baby Kate again this evening only for a couple of hours please, Nan?'

Sadie's nan replied softly, 'Of course I will dear and whatever it is that is making you become my darling dolly Sadie again then I'm game for encouraging this kiddo!' Sadie smiled at her nan and thanked her. Sadie's Nan teasingly said to Sadie, 'Oh, is it a boy?'

'No, Nan, it's not a boy, actually,' Sadie snapped back. Sadie wasn't ready to discuss her love life with her, as knowing her nan she would only then go onto ask if her boyfriend is the father of baby Kate. For Sadie this was to be buried and never discussed but for some reason the disgraceful subject just keeps popping up. Sadie's mind was in overdrive. What happens if her and Jack get serious and he wants her to tell him about her baby's father? Jack can never know! In fact no one can ever know! No one! The thought scared the life out of Sadie and she became fretful and agitated just thinking about the exposure of the dreaded disturbing disgusting secret that she begrudgingly held. How could she go from warm and calm one minute and then the next minute turn into an irrational withdrawn freak of her former self. This only made Sadie feel even more frustrated and emotional. Sadie walked from her nan's without saying a word. Sadie's nan didn't think anything of Sadie's strange behaviour she just put it down to her granddaughter being a teen.

# Nine

I woke to the smell of eggs and bacon. Yes Mr William White was cooking breakfast. Un-fucking-believable! Well what a turnout, the country lane scenario ended up with me tucked up in Will's three-bedroom apartment at the Dock Yard, in Chatham. Well you've never seen anything like it. The history alone smacks you in the face as soon as you enter the famous crowned arch, this is security at its best. The stone brickwork that you see takes you back at least a hundred years. The Maid's Quarters, The General's Office, The Dock Building, The Engine Rooms, The Ships and then every so often you see the bright red bricks from that of the modern build. The brickwork and the windows of the modern build do not compare to that of the wise, aged buildings that stand so strong amongst the innovation of our scrawny new builds. So compacted together are the new builds, slimmer than that of any old build.

William owned the building immediately to the right upon entrance through the golden arch. It was an amazing apartment split over several levels. The interior was immaculate. A pale grey carpet and grey stone covered the floors. Pure white walls only enhanced the space and Georgian sash windows donned this upmarket home. A very simple look with a grand masculine presence felt throughout. White bedding which was one hundred percent pure cotton. I knew this as there was no roughness like that of nylon. I had also spotted a little label on the side of the duvet cover that read 'by Yves Delorme' I wouldn't have had a clue who the designer was or even if he was a he, but what I did know was that William had chosen super expensive bedding. It wasn't just his clothes that were designer it was also his home.

Frankie would not be a happy bunny. I'm sure she doesn't own designer bedding. Apparently, the little squirrel, Will that is, only purchased this place a couple of years back. He says Frank has no clue of it and that I am certain of as Frank would indulge in this luxury and, believe me, this swanky pad would be worth shouting about. Although we had the most amazing sex when we got back to William's secret pad we also talked, like really talked, there were even times in our conversation that I thought I'm just going to tell him about Sadie! I soon bottled it! I actually think I could cause him to have a heart attack if I disclosed something so big after so long. However, Will did stress to me that he knew him and Frank would never be together forever. Of course he loves her. She is the mother of his children. End of. He stressed he always thought they would definitely grow apart once the children grew up. But never in a million years did he think she would screw around behind his back. Now he says that she has done him the biggest favour of his life as he has no guilt to feel. He can still be a good dad and provide for his children and 'at the same time be free of the lecherous cunt' as William liked to put it. He even told me that he thought she had been fucking around with his mate Matty Dobbs, albeit it was a long time ago and William never had any proof back then so he thought he was just being paranoid. However, Frankie has now confirmed to William that his initial thought of her playing around, combined with her latest shenanigans she, Frankie that is, is probably definitely guilty of fucking his mate Matty Dobbs.

William then said, 'Apparently Frank, when they were younger, like little kids, say eleven maybe twelve years old she was known as Franky for a finger.'

My curiosity got the better of me and innocently I asked, 'Why?'

To my utter dismay he replied through fits of giggles that, 'She often let four of the lads that they grew up with finger her one at a time.' I literally couldn't believe my ears. I didn't laugh. I was shocked and saddened for Frank that she obviously felt so needy and vulnerable to have allowed this to take place. I knew Frank never really had a normal upbringing but who did where we were from? But I now question what really went on in Frank's childhood to make her so sexual so young. Her mum was and still is the estate bike. I can only imagine the weirdos that she had wrapped around Frank as a child. I actually feel sick at the thought.

Will and I ate our breakfast on the terrace which was very setting for the scene. It was like I had completely deserted my own downtrodden and somewhat tiresome world and miraculously ended up in the world of my very own fantasy. It's like ecstasy. Well not that I have ever taken ecstasy but I imagine it gives you this phantasm feeling that I have been experiencing of late.

I had no clean clothes with me so I was lolling about stark naked. This was fine as we had no onlookers. I felt liberated and I did not want my time to end here with William White. William even disclosed some of his scandalous business arrangements to me in our heart to heart last night. I think the Remi Martin certainly encouraged Will's honesty the previous evening. For me the Remi helped me comprehend some of Will's wicked confessions. I could not switch off from some of the shocking shit that he revealed. The one thing that tormented me the most was his involvement in brothels. I had trouble accepting his drug-dealing ways but earning a profit on the sexual exploitation of vulnerable women made me angry at William. William tried his utmost to reassure me that he was not making anyone do anything they didn't want to do and he did try and reinforce that his brothel business was really just a way to protect the women that chose to live that life.

'Kate you've been lucky ma darling in the sense that you've never been exposed to such a world. But babe you wouldn't believe how many 'ave. And they earn a good living, live a good life for a few hours a week work. Some of these women had been stuck in factories for seventy hour weeks and could still barely exist. Some are students paying their way to a better life. Some are single parents trying to make ends meet. I say make it legal and it would be safer. But Kate I'm no one of real power so instead I look at it that these unfortunate souls and meself, I'm giving 'em a safer working environment and believe me Kate baby that is rare in this world of ours! My point is my girl don't frown upon me. I promise ya it's their choice, it's individual preference, Kate. No one is forced. Take a leaf out of Amsterdam! Kate, it really is only a man-made fucking law mate and sometimes they, those man-made laws, actually push the poorer further into poverty. Alright close your mouth now Kate! I know it's criminal activity, I know, but no rape or naughty murders go on at my houses! Who fucking knows what's right, a Kate! But again, nun a that naughty shit happens to any a me girls because we operate good Kate and not bad!'

I just listened. What could I say? Although William was able to diminish my annoyed mood with his hardness this was only short held. I couldn't help but question my own moral standing. William was my fantasy, my guilty pleasure, my daughter's undisclosed father and was this enough for me to forgive his faulty behaviour? I would ask myself, though, how another human can have such a detrimental impact on your thoughts when at the same time this same human is also able to positively ignite so many repressed emotions within you, allowing such joy?

Something I think would be simply described as life and truly living within it and not existing on the edge of it, like so many of us do. Ironic I know considering you would assume most criminals live their life on the edge, as such. But it's a mad, crazy and dysfunctional life that some of us lead. For me being a woman and finding a man that I find both sexually attractive, emotionally stimulating, with a shared mutual respect (a must), and finally a wholesome sex life and just being able to indulge in a deep connection with another being, I guess is the fuel for my own heightened existence. I am now realising that because of my own personal desires I seem to allow my very own righteous conscious to be ignorant to that of the imperfections of my man. Complex, I know. Why can it not just be simple?

William had to rush off after breakfast. Apparently one of his houses, or shall I say brothels, had been raided. The phone call that he received was from a woman, I could hear her foul mouth screeching loudly at William. William appeared very composed considering the current drama. He strode around his apartment naked whilst making calls to various wrong'uns. Much to my dismay the arrogant cocky confidence of the man only made William White more attractive to her. Surely though this type of man will eventually fall from his own immoral standing, I thought. In my heart of hearts I wanted so much to believe that William was a good man however, he wasn't giving me much hope right now. William did not take any of his cars, he was picked up in a brand new shiny red Mercedes. The car had blacked out windows so I couldn't even get a glimpse of who was driving, which only agitated me more.

Sometimes William was so open and relaxed with me and then as quickly as I became his other limb as such I was amputated just as fast. William had this knack of shutting down on me. The coldness I felt when William went into business mode was like that of being dumped, rejected and ignored. He may as well be entertaining another woman because that's how William made me feel when he was on business. I hated myself for being so needy. Needy is something I'm not. Well I wasn't until William White had come along and captured me in his web and allowed me a glimpse of his underworld skulduggery.

The whole journey back home, I cried. I was praying the taxi driver could not see my pathetic tears spilling down my face. Sunglasses were a godsend for an emotional woman, ironically it was probably a fucking man who invented them, I thought. What had I got myself into? That's all that was whirling around in my head. As I pulled up in the taxi I saw Fiona chatting outside her front gate to some random. The last thing I needed right now was an interrogation from Fiona.

## Ten

Frankie was called Frankie Twirp, although she would often tell people she was Frankie White. The fact was, she was just dreaming, as Frankie had never been married and it was looking very unlikely that she would ever become a married Mrs.

Frankie was an only child from a single parent background, her father was shot when she was just two years old. Rumour has it Frankie's mother and her boyfriend at the time set the whole shooting up. Frankie is not shy to this particular version. However, her mother has always insisted that her father was an addict and got in with the wrong kind. The problem Frankie has with her mother's version of events regarding her father's so-called addiction is because when Frankie was around the age of thirteen she found her father's toxicology report and it was completely free of drugs. So even though Frankie was not deemed the most academic she certainly was not stupid and knew her mother was a liar.

However, Frankie has only ever had her mother, no father, no grandparents, no brothers or sisters, no aunts no uncles and no cousins, a very lonely person was Frankie Twirp. It would seem for the sake of having a blood relative Frankie has suppressed the fact her mother may well be responsible for her own father's death. Maureen Twirp, Frankie's mum, was a hard-faced woman. She had short, boy-like, bleached blonde hair that always donned black greasy roots, as tall as a giraffe with a hench-like figure, slim build not roly-poly fat but a big structured strong woman with lots of tacky tattoos.

Frankie was similar to her mother facially, nonetheless a much more slender and shorter feminine-looking version. They both had big strong Roman noses, small squinty blue eyes and flat thin lips. Well, Frankie used to have thin lips until she found a new best friend called collagen, she used to own small tits like her mother until she was introduced to breast enlargement, obviously all at the expense of Mr William White.

Maureen Twirp was the type of woman who would openly and proudly tell all and sundry that she ran a massage parlour over in Gillingham. She had no shame did old Maureen and obviously no discretion. All said and done Maureen loved her grandsons and spoilt them all rotten. I think this show of love helped Frankie forgive her mother's treacherous ways. Truth be told Maureen got Frankie on the game from the age of eleven. It was the day Frankie started her period that Maureen felt fit to tell her daughter about sex. Maureen explained what her duty was and now that she had become a woman she must earn her own crust. Those indecent disgusting shocking words that fell from her mother's lips the day Frankie became a proper woman would haunt Frank forever.

'Just ya remember my girl ya fanny's worth fifty notes, ya mouth's worth twenty notes and if ya wanting a bum bonus that will get ya a oner my girl! And remember don't let no one take advantage of ya thick nature!' Obviously Frankie had never disclosed this to a single person. She carried this information around with her for longer than thirty years. There were many times her punters had been in her company unexpectedly. Like the time she had a meeting with Will Jnr's head teacher. The embarrassment was felt by both parties. Needless to say though Will J was given an easy time throughout the rest of his primary education and Will J was an absolute bastard child. Will J was the kind of kid other parents abhorred. He would cut the other kids' hair, flick paint over kids' clothes, put one poor kid's head down the toilet. Will J was a delinquent.

Then there was the time that Frank was visiting her friend and her friend's dad happened to be there as well, yes another extremely awkward shameful moment. Frank told herself they were her shamefucks! The worst and most uncomfortable was the first time she met William White's father. Throughout the whole of Frankie and William's relationship his father was the worst of the shamefucks that Frankie had ever encountered. He was a torturous cunt who always bribed Frankie for sexual favours. His name funny enough was William too, a family tradition. He loved to get Frankie at family gatherings. It was the thrill. The predictability was so predictable. Old Father White always waited for everyone to be half-cut or drunk as skunks before he made his move. Always in the family bathroom. Always a blow job and a finger up his arse. He would force-feed his cock to Frankie at any opportunity. Once and only once did old man Will come to Frank's house when she was alone. It was way before the two youngest were born. That was the first time Frankie was made to have sex with his dog. Old man Will was one warped man. Frankie had to endure this particular sex favourite off the twisted old cunt until he died, which was only two years ago. She couldn't hide her happiness at his funeral. She got off her face and dedicated a song to him. 'Always look on the bright side of life.' Oh and Frankie Twirp sang with exasperation that day.

'Oi ya little bastards get ya arses in ere!' screamed Frankie at her two youngest. Frankie had stayed at her mum's for a few weeks. The only reason Frankie returned back home was because her mother was winging about money. The words Frankie's mother had said to her just kept spinning around in her head. 'You silly little whore don't think ya can slob round 'ere all fucking goddamn day and think ya gonna get a free fucking ride! I got a nice little punter lined up for you! Be ready at nine this evening or fuck off ya lazy ponce.' Frank had stared at her mother in disbelief. It took her back to that day she became a woman.

Maureen Twirp walked casually from the house as if wishing her daughter a good day. The pang Frankie felt when she thought of those cold love moments still physically hurt. How can a mother get it so wrong?

Maureen Twirp would literally screw her own flesh and blood for a fiver. Frank obviously chose the latter of her mother's offer. However, at points, the temptation of some extra cash did entice Frankie's thoughts and provoke her conscience. Nevertheless, the thought of putting her body through such torture let alone the fact she would probably lose her mind as well, she quickly dismissed that seedy thought of earning a bit of extra cash.

Frank had only seen Will a few times and that was when he came for the kids and then dropped them back off. Will would look straight through her, even though she would have made her very best efforts to get his attention. It had been nearly three months now and nothing Frankie tried helped her depressed state. She knew in her heart of hearts she had lost William forever. If only she hadn't wanted revenge on all his coke whores she would still be living her life in abundance. It was a struggle not just emotionally but financially Frankie was also screwed although she got an extra few hundred pounds a month in disability living allowance for her son John Boy for his ADHD. Yet that barely covered her cocaine addiction. She is actually considering going down the disability route for herself as 'there's no way she can go and get a fucking job', as Frankie liked to put it. The thought scared the life out of Frankie. She had no qualifications and 'the only fucking work experience she possessed was sucking and sitting on cock' again as Frankie liked to say it.

Frankie just couldn't decide whether she should pursue

the mental health path or exaggerate her bad back or even tell them she has a cocaine addiction, she did hear they give more money to addicts than single mums. Frankie would have to check with some of her pals which one gave the most money. The thing is, Frankie knows she only really has disability living allowance for John Boy until he reaches sixteen. John Boy will be thirteen next month, this gives her three years to push for her own disability living allowance. Frankie doesn't not know which way to turn.

She took the boys to school and went to McDonald's to meet her friend Jodie. Apparently Frankie's mate Jodie is on her arse too and can't even afford to feed her kids at the minute.

'Single parents are mugged right off, give more fucking dollar to the fucking junkies down the high street than they do us,' Jodie sobbed to Frankie over a sausage McMuffin. Jodie told Frank, 'You'd never fucking believe it Frank I only read online that single mums have kids of their own just for the money and the house. I aint even got a fucking house Frank me and the four kids are crammed up in a damp-ridden fucking poxy over-priced private renter's two-bed flat!' Jodie was getting angry at this point and getting louder. 'It's a fucking joke though Frank, seriously, fuckin try living on fifty quid for yourself and fifty quid a week for each fucking dadless kid! And then they take my rent back out of that and council tax! Frank it's killing me, literally we are potless. I 'ave just over five quid a day for a bit of food, the gas and electric lives on the emergency, and then there's everything else! I aint even got no fridge at the minute, it's been leaking water for the last six months and now its hotter than the kitchen itself.' Jodie was now sobbing, she was uncontrollable.

Frankie gave her friend a cuddle, she didn't care that they were sat in the middle of McDonald's. Frankie, although she came across a hard-faced careless mouthy bitch, she actually had the biggest heart and would do anything for her friends. And normally when Frank was with Will she would have one hundred percent slipped her desperate mate at least a few hundred pounds for a fridge and some food. However Frank had no suggestions this time. She herself was struggling too. Her only advice for her friend was.

'You need to get yerself on the sick, Jode.' Or sell your minge and your soul at the same time. Frank thought the latter rather than saying it aloud. Frankie never discussed her prostitution days with her friends or anyone other than her sick cunt of a mother. At that very same moment Frank did think about her mother. Was she as sick as she had thought all these years or was she just as desperate as Jodie here? Anyway Jodie was totally against the sick route. She was convinced social services would take her kids if she claimed a false sickness. Frank thought this was a naïve response even from Jodie. Well, in all fairness, Jodie was only twenty- one. Clearly social services only take the kids when there is serious neglect. Frank was certain of this as she'd had social services around her house every other week when she was a kid and they did fuck all to stop the nonces coming to mishandle her childhood. Frankie dismissed her disturbing creepy thoughts.

From personal experience Frankie had no faith in social services, in fact Frankie was of the belief that half of them were only there to abuse their position of power. This cringed Frank and she sat silently. Jodie then shocked the fuck out of Frank.

'I have thought about escorting, Frank, one of my mates Joel does it, she earns a wedge, Frank.' Jodie said this in a desperate but hopeful tone. Frank advised Jodie against this but also said that if she did need a contact she knew a trustworthy source. Frank did not ever think she would be recommending her mother's illicit services to anyone, let alone a friend. However, Frank was thinking at least she knows her mother will keep Jodie safe and her young desperate friend won't at any point end up being found cut up in some council bin.

## Eleven

Sadie was overjoyed as her mum had managed to get her a week's work experience at the Brooke Theatre in Chatham. The theatre for Sadie was like the missing part of her soul. When she was little just before she was robbed of her childhood and obviously her virginity, Sadie lived for the theatre and her dancing. Sadie went three times a week. Twice to the Brooke Theatre and once a week to the Hook. The Hook was the local community centre on the edge of the council estate where Sadie lived. Sadie had attended the humble dance school since she was three years old. Sadie had missed her dancing and acting and hadn't realised just how much until she was back at the Brooke doing her work experience. The building itself made Sadie get goose bumps. The actual stage and theatre gave Sadie an immense natural buzz.

Sadie was feeling more and more like her old self and actually for once had a ray of hope for a happy untainted future. Baby Kate was a beautiful bonny seven-month- old baby now and was becoming a cheeky little character. Sadie felt her life at this moment in time was hers again, she had been seeing lots more of Jack and he now knew about baby Kate and he was absolutely fine. Actually Jack had only asked once about baby Kate's father. However, from Sadie's response, Jack never felt the need to ask again. Sadie told Jack that baby Kate's father was dead. Jack had no reason to question this. Maybe if Jack had been a little older and more mature he would have most definitely questioned Sadie more about baby Kate's father's death. However innocence proved at this time to have worked in Sadie's favour.

Sadie decided that she was going to ask her mother if she would look after the baby so she could go back to dancing and acting classes. The work experience was the most amazing week for Sadie and of course her mum would juggle her already manic schedule to allow Sadie to pursue something that makes her feel so happy again. The fact it will also certainly enhance Sadie's chances of getting into university to study theatre and dance means, of course her mum will say yes. It's a no brainer, thought Sadie.

University has always been a dream for Sadie. Even Sadie herself never thought she would have had the heart, let alone the opportunity, to pursue her dream after having her baby so young. Life, though, for Sadie right now was looking bright. Sadie was finally turning her back on the negatives and embracing the positives. She was all too aware of how great her mum had been and if it were not for her mum being so supportive, Sadie would never have had the confidence to return to school let alone embark on her dreams. Sadie knew she had matured since that awful evening when she was set upon. She didn't quite know if it was because she had in effect had sex or was it because the way she had experienced it or was it now because she had a baby? Either way Sadie knew that she had grown up overnight. The world she once upon a time perceived is so dramatically differently now. Everywhere Sadie went she felt was a potential risk. Sadie never felt safe being alone anymore but hoped in time that this would fade just like the memories of that night. She prays to forget nightly and she still asks herself how had she ever so wickedly encountered something so disturbingly dark?

Her mum would now be her personal taxi, for how long Sadie did not know. Sadie had been at bit wayward after the birth of baby Kate but now she no longer needed alcohol to drown out her existence. Her studies, baby Kate and Jack were more than enough for Sadie to find some sort of contentment after so much carnage. Jack was round this evening and Sadie was cooking him some pasta and cheese. Sadie was learning her way around a cooker but she wasn't the most adventurous in that area. However she was looking forward to some time with just her Jack and baby Kate, her mother was going to see Laney, and Sadie felt grown up, as her mother was leaving them alone for the evening as a family. Her mother would have never left Sadie alone with a boy a year ago.

How in just one year can so much change? A whole life, a whole new being, a whole new set of rules and a whole new life meaning! Sadie sometimes pinched herself to see if she was just trapped in some nightmare dream and she would wake back up into her happy innocent little life when pretty much dollies, dancing and daydreaming were her only concern, and not being a mum. The way Sadie's life was unfolding was not in her plan. Sadie was all about education. Marriage and babies were far from her girly thoughts. Sex, however, was not even a thought let alone a consideration.

Sadie looks back now and although some of the more popular girls in her year said they had been fingered and even a couple apparently had had sex, she didn't really believe them and thought that they were just seeking sexual attention. Attention Sadie was not at all into. Sadie was quite a young twelve-year-old. She had still slept with her favourite Cinderella and Snow White soft toys right up until she had had baby Kate, obviously they were not appropriate to sleep with anymore. Sadie found baby Kate was to be her knew cuddly comfort. Jack however, still top and tailed with Sadie and he was absolutely fine with this and never pushed for Sadie to be intimate with him. Jack had become Sadie's new best friend. Although it would appear he would one day expect more and Sadie just didn't know if she could ever give herself to anyone ever again?

# Twelve

I was at Will's, on the balcony, wrapped in my chunky knit navy cardigan and smoking a J laying on a lounger, enjoying the cool evening that lay very still and tranquil. Bill Withers and his classic 'Ain't no Sunshine When She's Gone' was blaring out of the teeny tiny speakers which were suspended from the wall of the apartment. This crazy design gave the effect that they were floating and the blue illumination that shone from them gave the appearance of delicate mood lighting. I liked this modern state of the art technology.

Will was in his office sorting business. It was early on a Friday evening and there certainly was a premature winter chill in the air. It was only just October and all the leaves from the trees and the petals from the flowers had started to turn and fall. I'd had a horrendous week – I failed my first trimester at college. I was gutted but felt this did not reflect my academic ability. It was purely down to putting my daughter and granddaughter first. I had pretty much become a mother again now that Sadie had returned to her dancing and drama classes. It seemed I'd neglected my own studies for the sake of my daughter's own academic achievements and future. All this extra responsibility that had been directed my way was fitted in and around my own cleaning jobs which consisted of fifteen houses a week plus my own housework. I was exhausted.

College was left on the back burner. I certainly couldn't have given up my cleaning! But hey it's just the normal fucking bullshit that comes with being a fucking jack jona single arse mumma. This is exactly how I would regularly describe the burdens of my world! 'A constant catch 22.' I can't even take on any more cleans because the DWP will just deduct most of it back from me, then I'll be worse off! Life sometimes just kicked the arse out of me!

I'd stopped smoking weed years ago but the last couple of weeks with all the crazy stress and failings at college I'd sneakily been having a J most evenings just to relax and somehow try and switch off. Life was a little prettier after smoking a J. Obviously my family don't know about my enjoyment for cannabis. Jeez, fuck that! My mother would write me off as the biggest druggy ever! This evening, I feel that this is certainly the case for my life right now. That feeling that everything is much prettier than it really is, helps towards me feeling less fucking bogged down. So for now I indulge in my guilty pleasure 'The green man.'

Sadie was at home with Jack and baby Kate. Those two seemed to be getting on great, I thought. Jack had certainly brought a spark back into my little girl's world and this was an achievement in itself as I never thought I'd ever see Sadie's eyes shine again but they weren't just shining right now they were dancing.

Ever since Sadie fell pregnant she had lost her spark but I could see that the spark has certainly come back to her and re-ignited my daughter's dreams and joy of life. Sadie always insisted she never knew she was pregnant.

I certainly never ever in a million years would have thought that my thirteen-year-old daughter could possibly be pregnant. Not my baby girl. I had much bigger and better aspirations for my Sadie. Surely this would be any mother's nightmare. Of course as a mother I noticed a change, shall we say a withdrawal. However I always put it down to Sadie being a teen and her absent father. I noticed the weight more than her moods but never wanted to make a point about it. As the last thing I ever wanted was an unnecessary anorexic on her hands. The thing was, I had once known a girl who had suffered with anorexia and the poor girl said it was triggered by her own father taking the piss out of her puppy fat. Therefore I was all too aware not to mention the word 'fat' or 'overweight' to a teenage girl, and certainly not to my own daughter. Hence we didn't find out Sadie was pregnant until she was seven months gone. We now know that was the first time Sadie had first experienced Braxton Hicks. I will never forget that moment to be honest, nor will my daughter. I was reading the Sunday papers lazing on the sofa listening to one of my favourite singers, Madonna, when Sadie came running in screaming there must be an alien in her tummy as it's moving and it hurt like hell. I was used to this kind of hypochondriac drama from my daughter so was really just thinking here we go again, nothing a paracetamol won't fix. Then to my utter dismay Sadie exposed her tummy. I actually screamed and shouted, 'what the fuck, Sade? I don't think that's no fucking alien! You stupid girl.' I remember the tears from both me and Sadie. The big fat sobs of disappointment and delusion were beyond that of any hope of happiness. Ironically Madonna's 'Papa Don't Preach' sang away. Still now that song provokes me and sends my whole body into goose bumps. It's amazing what music does for the senses.

That day, for me, felt like I was living another life. My precious baby so tainted. But all said and done baby Kate had brought so much hope and happiness into all of our worlds. Albeit we are still none the wiser who baby Kate's father is and I am far too scared to upset the apple cart at the moment certainly whilst Sadie is in such a great place, It will keep.

William soon interrupted my stoned normally locked away subconscious. He almost immediately started slipping his hand up my skirt and at the same time with his other hand was grabbing hold of my hair and then started kissing and caressing me so erotically I felt myself breath him in deeply. The actual physical senses that William evokes within me is sometimes indescribable. I often feel like I go to another realm when we are embodied together. His muscles in his legs, chest, arms and back were solid. He's as hard as steel. I was in awe of William and the more time we were spending together I was almost sure I was once again stupidly and crazily in love with him. However, I would never admit to this. I was sure that as soon as I admitted this theory to myself or to anyone else it would have to end. For one, I can't let a man in my world for fear of hurt. I have analysed this fucked up relationship cycle of mine. For many hours me and my friends would discuss the doomed relationship subject: why don't you let your guard down? You can't be frozen forever, Miss Andrews! Someone will eventually melt you! You won't find love sitting in! Loneliness will be the death of you! These were just some of my friends' taunts! 'To be quite honest with you my dear ladies,' I would say in a strong direct manner, 'I have never really felt love from a man and I actually think I don't really know how to show love and if and whenever I have thought that it may be love, I seem to just freeze up.'

The tears always sprang to my eyes even when I would think about this let alone when I said this fact out loud. Me and my friends came to the conclusion that because I had never had the love of a father, a grandfather nor a father figure of any sort that I must be dumb to loving a man. Then there was this massive fear of rejection. And although Will didn't realise it he had already rejected me before. However I was now secretly hoping that Will would be the one to educate my dumbness around loving a man and help me with my rejection issues.

Me and William were soon disturbed. The front door was being pounded in and the screams of a woman were clearly heard. William coldly told me to stay where I was. I would normally rebel against a man's order. However I did as I was told. Although I was thinking what the fuck and who the fuck could that be? I knew it wasn't Frankie, jeez, I had known that girl long enough and had heard her loud chavvy mouth for years to recognise if it were Frankie. With that thought in mind, the next thing a young, say, twenty-five-year-old curly red-haired woman walked onto the balcony screaming her mouth off at me.

'So you're his new fucking piece are ya?' This woman was wild. 'You do realise luv I been fucking the man for the last ten year!' The words that were being screamed at me from this unknown mad red creature made me feel like a bulldozer was digging out at my guts, a hammer was smashing at my head, and my poor pure heart felt like that of a wrung-out, old, dirty dishcloth. Amazing how the bodily senses were reacting quicker than my mind.

The physical pain I felt at William's infidelity was as enraptured as the sex I'd had with him. For me, the shame of being another meaningless fuck was all too much too bear. The bullshit I had falsely endured. The bile was now rising in my throat. Fuck, I need to get out of here. All the while Will was trying to get the wild red banshee out, without hurting her of course. Always the fucking gent! I want to wring her neck was another thought that sprang to my mind. She has just maliciously and miraculously mangled my already fragile heart. I felt that my whole body must be actually bleeding from the unexpected blunt blow of the truth, I actually felt faint. It was literally like the life was draining away from me. She, the red demon that is, was all arms and legs and William was struggling to wrestle with the young red-haired plaything that he had so secretly acquired.

Will was trying his hardest to remove the juvenile wild red thing, she kept holding onto door frames with her long slender varnished hands and using her feet as stop stumps at every opportunity. She seemed impossible. I grabbed my bag and keys and left. Down the stairs, running as fast as my tears were flowing, and out the front door I ran.

All the while Will was shouting, 'Please babe let me explain! Please Kate. Please just hear me out!' I was in my car. Tracey Chapman's 'Give Me One Reason' was blaring away. I was an emotional wreck. I actually couldn't drive for fear of crashing. I was in such a state I ended up pulling into the Command Public House car park. I didn't notice the time until I heard it on the radio - 'the eleven o'clock news.' Surely I hadn't been sitting here for over four hours. I'd lost all sense of time.

Gathering my thoughts together and enticing them back into the present time felt totally impossible. The pain I felt within, my gut was actually twisting and knotting to the point I had to open the door on more than several occasions as I couldn't stop the vomiting. I could not believe the events of the evening. Those words the red-haired girl was shouting off were buzzing through me making me feel wired. Ten fucking years, she would have been fresh out of school, probably got a fucking kid with her as well, the piece of shit cunt that he is! I was fuelled with mad thoughts. My phone was buzzing away. I looked down and the phone was flashing up at her 'Laney two'. However it wasn't Laney at all she was my disguise for Will. That's where I said I stayed every time I stayed out with Will. Laney was a silent alibi as such. Terrible of me really, considering Laney's recent devoted declaration. My own subconscious was niggling away at my reality. I know if you wrong someone you will be wronged. Surely it was just the way of the world. Karma and that. Whatever modern term is used you get the point. Treat others as you wish to be treated. I knew in my heart of hearts that my short burst of love that I had experienced with Will was at the expense of another's heartache and therefore I knew that I could never have ever been truly happy with William White. Although this did not stop the snot and tears.

# Thirteen

The next few weeks went by in a blur. What with work, Sadie and baby Kate there was really no time for me to dwell. William had tried calling a few times the first week. However he soon gave up. That just made me think what we had didn't run that deep for William.

'I had to shut down, I can't cope with developing feelings for a man at the best of times. I feel so fucking rejected and worthless,' I cried to Sadie.

I knew I shouldn't have been having this conversation with Sadie but I had indulged in too many glasses of pinot. Therefore the alcohol meant I couldn't hide my loss and emotion. I never disclosed who the man was but just told Sadie, 'He is just a man from work.'

Sadie was a wise young lady. 'Oh, Mum you'll be fine you're a tough cookie and if he is worth you, it will be yeah, whatever's meant to be will be, my dear mother!' said Sadie in a matter of fact tone.

'The transition that you my baby girl has had to adapt to has been insane, but my beautiful little dolly I'm so fucking goddamn proud of you,' I said admiringly and with a slur to Sadie whilst at the same time pulling her in for a cuddle. Over the last couple of months we had become such close friends and seemed to have built a bond that was so strong no one and nothing could ever break it. Sadie had grown into a mature, level-headed beautiful young woman. Sometimes I actually thought Sadie was more sagacious than I could ever be at her age. Sadie had come into her own. I know a lot of this is to do with her going back to her dancing and acting. And let's not forget Jack, he has certainly had an amazing impact on Sadie enjoying life again too.

For some reason I knew that as long as Sadie has her way at the theatre she will always be ok. Man or no man. Sadie shows spirit and for me that is highlighted through my daughter's perspective of a man. Sadie would never be the type of woman to revolve her world around a man. Sadie had far too many other passions to conquer in her life and a man certainly wasn't the be all and end all for Sadie.

'Let a man follow you follow your dreams, Mum,' said Sadie in a firm tone. 'And if the cock is worth it mother, he will do just that! Follow you that is, Mum!' Sadie suddenly spun into a fit of giggles whilst trying to say. 'You didn't moan at me for saying cock! That's gotta be the first a ma, me not being told off for swearing.' Sadie seemed to be trying to lift her mother's spirit.

I stared at my daughter hard and wasn't really listening to her and before I could think I blurted out, 'Baby please tell me, your mum, who the father is.' I just said it, I didn't even think about it, it just came out. I wanted to kick myself for it as soon as those few words left my lips. I knew in my heart this conversation wasn't going to end well.

'Not now, Mum, maybe one day maybe I will tell you but not now,' responded Sadie sadly. I couldn't control myself and pushed my daughter some more.

'Surely, my dolly, it can't be that bad that you can't even tell your own mother.'

'Actually, Mum, I thought my own father being dead was the worst thing ever for a little girl to grow up with or should I say without? But no actually I would do anything for my baby's dad to be dead! And that's not even the best bit. Yes I know my baby was born the same fucking day my own father faced his own death! Yes, my dear mother, I hadn't missed that fact, not that you have had the decency to even speak to me about it! And you know what, I didn't want to bring it up cause I didn't want to upset you, yes fucking upset you! At the end of the day I look at that as my good omen, Mum, mine! So don't go wasting your tears over feeling guilty on me!' screamed Sadie at me.

I was stunned into complete silence. I felt so gutted and cross with myself. Why did I have to go and bring the whole 'who's the daddy' subject up? But also why is it such a secret? And why can't my dear daughter trust me enough to just disclose the father of baby Kate? I felt helpless and useless as well as having a bruised heart, and now this. I did no more than sob at the kitchen table. But I could only blame myself, I was responsible for fucking up my daughter by telling her that her father was dead, when in fact her dear dead father had been living right next door to her for pretty much her whole goddamn life.

Oh and the fucking 24th of March had a lot to answer for! It was, in fact, the day I first had an abortion, yes William White was the father. It wasn't long after my abortion that I fell pregnant with Sadie but I was adamant I would not have another abortion and kill another of my unborn babies. Therefore I thought it would be an appropriate date for the false death of Sadie's father. An omen and that! The thought Sadie ever found out about my terrible lies scared the life out of me. How could any child forgive their own mother for depriving them of a father? When all is said and done, William White was a fucking good father which in turn only added to my guilt.

It was Monday morning and I was due at work but couldn't face it and phoned in sick. My head was banging. I looked out of the window first thing and I actually said out loud, 'Fuck that!'. It was late November and the weather was true to its word. A typical English morning for this time of year. Thick blocks of frozen ice were stuck to the cars, the roofs of the houses were coated in a sparkling blanket of white frost, all the chimneys were smoking away, the large, frosty, bare, brown trees stood so strong yet looked so baron, and what with my fuzzy head and dodgy tummy this was enough for me to succumb to the weather and take pity within the comfort of my warm lonely bed.

I thought that the cold bright white of the outside that I was witness to this morning was a perfect reflection of how I felt right now, frozen. What with the terrible hangover I was experiencing and the crazy sub-zero world that seemed to be imposing in on me this chilly winter morning, there was no way I was going on my normal mad maid mission today. Baby Kate can stay at home with me today, I thought, as I wrapped myself deep under the duvet. Sadie had poked her head into my room and just said that she was leaving and that baby Kate was still sleeping. I knew Sadie was being offish as she asked nothing about why I was not going to work, there wasn't even a 'bye', let alone a 'love you'. Me and baby Kate didn't wake until gone ten. We only woke because Frankie was banging the door down and shouting out at the top of her lungs.

'Kate, Kate are you home?' Frank must've been out the front for at least five minutes yelling her big fat mouth off.

'Obviously I'm fucking home you dumb fuck. My car's outside, however, I'm sleeping!' I mumbled to myself. It was at that point I looked at the clock which read ten thirty-three. My immediate thought was the baby. I jumped up so quickly and in my shocked state ran into baby Kate's room to check she was ok.

On entering the baby's room I went flying on a plastic pink glittery glow ball. It was ironic I guess the joy of the baby's toy had managed to trip me up and send me flying. I ended up smashing my chin on the chest of drawers and found myself flat-faced squashed into the cot bars, which baby Kate found super funny. She was laughing hysterically at her nan's unfortunate fall. Blood was dripping everywhere. The cream carpet was now a pink spotted cream carpet. Another job I will have to sort out at some point today, carpet cleaning, I thought to myself and then looked at my granddaughter and lovingly said, 'Oh, baby I wonder how long you have been awake just cooing away letting me sleep. Oh, Nanny does love you.' I absolutely adored my unexpected granddaughter. I quickly picked her up and gave her lots of squeezes and cuddles and went and answered the door to Frankie.

'What you doing 'ome ya little skiver?' bellowed Frankie. Frankie never ceased to amaze me with her sarcastic manner. The girl had never done a day's graft in her life and had the audacity to insinuate I was a lazy dosser. I would never say my thoughts to Frankie, it would cause too much drama and I couldn't be bothered with small-minded people and their ignorant insults. Sometimes things are best left unsaid, I knew this all too well. However I sarcastically did say to Frankie,

'No Frank it's my day off. I have actually just worked fifteen days straight. My first day off was yesterday and to be honest I feel fucked!' Stick that in your pipe and smoke it Frankie Twirp, I thought, with a pang of bitterness.

Frank seemed to blah blah on about herself as usual. How her Will J is getting a hard time in jail. 'And big Will needs to have a fucking word with some of his cronies to sort the shit cunts out!' Frank sounded protective although it was probably just another way of trying to get William's attention. Who gives a shit was what I was secretly thinking. Fucking little wrong'un anyway.

'I'm sure if Will knew his boy was in trouble, Frank, he

wouldn't sit back and do jack shit, mate,' I defensively replied to Frankie. I busied myself making coffee and getting the baby's breakfast. However I was wishing I could smoke a blazing J right now and drown Frank and her fucking whining right out. Then I realised I actually hadn't had a J since I saw William last and god that was two months ago now. There she goes again, on on on about her Willy, Frank was obsessed. Then Frank went on to say that she was hoping Will would be coming round later as it's Josh's first birthday.

I embarrassingly responded, 'Oh fuck Frank, I'm so sorry! I totally forgot that it was Josh's birthday, gosh I feel terrible! I'll pop out shortly and treat him.'

'Don't be silly Kate he's alright he don't even know, the little bastard! He had me up all fucking night with his winging and moaning! Must be his teeth for fuck's sake, though the poor little fucker's still not got a friggin' tooth in his head! They need to fucking hurry up, a mate!' replied Frank bluntly, and all the while looking at Josh with an unfortunate stare.

I did no more than go and pick the little boy up and give him a cuddle and a birthday kiss. Josh was a dear little boy, such a lovely nature and he always played lovely with baby Kate. Always showing her toys whilst she sat in her high chair eager for his attention. And Josh was never violent towards her. Love him. Oh and Jesus, Josh looked like his dad too. There was certainly no denying him, he really was the spit of his male maker.

Then Frankie started blasting on about how she was on her period and, 'Fucking hell Kate I'm on so heavy it's like a fucking red sea Tsunami down there.' I knew Frank was funny and certainly loved her way with words. However the subject also made me question when my last period was. I tried to do this, however, with Frankie banging, on I felt myself getting a bit agitated at not being able to recall my last period. All I could think was fuck, fuck, fuck, when the fuck was my period?

Frank was looking at me blank-faced saying, 'What do you think Kate?' I was put on the spot and hadn't got a clue what Frank was asking.

'Well to be honest Frank just take one step at a time, try not to think too far ahead and things whatever they are they will work themselves out!' Bang, I thought, I had managed to respond to my friend without being totally way off track for Frank to even notice. I actually wanted to high-five myself. However the words come back almost immediately fuck, fuck, my period when were you? They, those words, tortured me for the rest of the day. I was beside myself.

Frank managed to get me to watch Josh whilst she went and had a blow dry and got her nails done. Anyone would think it was Frank's birthday, but no it wasn't that, Frankie was just trying to make her very best efforts to get William's attention. Frankie had lost over a stone in weight and felt really good about herself. She was hoping William would notice. Although Frankie had always had issues with her weight, there really was no need, there was nothing of her anyway. Frank certainly showed traits of someone with an eating disorder. There was a time when Frankie lived off cocaine, coffee and the occasional bit of toast. Well actually it now seems Frankie has reverted back to those ways - 'her caffeine and coke-fuelled ways' - what with her weight plummeting so quickly it doesn't take a psychologist to work that out.

Frankie was fuming by the time she had got back to my house to pick Josh up.

'He is some sort of cunt!' shouted Frank as soon as I opened the door. I obviously knew Frank meant Will. Not that I had a chance to ask as Frankie was in a mad rage spewing verbal crap.

'Silly old coke head cunt, how can he blow his own baby boy out on his first birthday? I want to fucking kill him. I bet he is with his little whore. Reckons he's got business he can't ignore, drug-dealing mother's cunt!' Frank was wild and continued her rage for the entire two hours that she sat in my house. I made coffee and nodded where and when appropriate. I actually couldn't believe that both parents couldn't actually give a flying fuck that it's their little boy's first birthday. Frank ended up going out and getting completely blind drunk. I looked after the boys for her.

As it was Josh's birthday and I had been paid today there was a little bit of extra cash. I could afford to take Sadie, baby Kate and Frank and William's boys for a KFC. The children seemed happy even baby Kate was eating the chicken and gravy.

Sadie had come home in a lovely mood and seemed to have forgiven me for the previous night's dilemma of our 'who's the daddy?' conversation. I ended up putting the two boys in my bed and made a bed up on the sofa for myself. I felt absolutely exhausted as I sunk into my big, soft, grey sofa and indulged in the silence that prevailed. However this moment of bliss was soon invaded. The day's events had slowly crept back into my conscience and bang it had come back to me, those dreaded words, when was my period due? I hadn't had to worry about when my period was due for over three years. I sometimes couldn't believe it myself! Why I hadn't indulged in sex for that long god only knows. Some would say it's self-torture to deprive oneself of such a very much needed necessity, like food, water and air, sex is a must in order for the human brain to function normally and it certainly helps to shut out that feeling of discontentment.

The legend DH Lawrence taught me much about sex and a happy existence. And with this in mind I knew that I had deprived myself for far too long, I almost became detached, and the lonely orgasm became a far too regular act for me. I knew that masturbation was certainly a substitute for a lover and that the lonely orgasm should not be used as a substitute for a lover as it will never properly fulfil the soul as a lover may, and that masturbation should only be used as an adventurous bonus! Only I was now certain of my theory about the 'onesome' and lovers, as I now realised, I had not only chosen to be celibate for so long but I chose to reject any male attention as I was and had been in love with only one man for over sixteen years.

The only reason I acknowledged or even realised my own suppression is because of my recent sexual encounters with William, which obviously provoked my love for him and my need for him and in turn this has made me see that a lonely orgasm is ok now and again but not for long periods of time as there is no chance of ever feeling that mind-blowing love on your own but only with a lover! Albeit a long-term or temporary sexual encounter has got to be better than a 'onesome'. As long as there is chemistry there is passion and it should be indulged not ignored, I thought deeply. It's not like your grave will be engraved with all your sweet little fucks! Why society tarnishes this behaviour I don't know! As long as you're single fucking mingle! Dionysus would frown upon us frigid rigid creatures of the millennia! I knew I was pregnant. Although I've had no sickness, my breasts however, have doubled in size and if I'm honest my period is actually six to eight weeks late. Fuck, was the only thing that sprang to mind!

## Fourteen

It was Christmas Eve and Frankie was off her face celebrating the festivities on a night out in Rochester – meaning copious amounts of cocaine and alcohol fuelled Frankie's body. Frankie thought she looked hot. Her hair was overdue a bleaching, her roots were halfway down her head. She wore a tight, lycra, white dress and Kurt Geiger white stilettos. Bright red lipstick donned her ever so plumped up lips. Cocaine powdered her nostrils. Frank had given up on William. He was stone cold towards her.

Frank was now seeing a few men. Tom Crane being one of them. Fiona would hit the roof if she ever found out. Truth be known Fiona could not stand Frankie. Fiona says, 'Frankie is a wrong'un and you know how I know this girl? Cause her kids don't come first her fucking pussy and nose does.'

The thing is Frankie is not shy who she tells about her drug and sex antics. Frankie is often standing out the front telling all and sundry who she is fucking. It would seem Frank is on a destructive path and doing anything and everything to get William's attention albeit good or bad. The thing is Tom is a good, proper old-fashioned gent and will spoil Frank rotten and we all know Frank will abuse Tom's good nature. Don't get me wrong, Tom is no muppet when it comes to drugs, money and business as such, but when Tom has a bit of fluff, which is rare, he certainly wears his rose-tinted glasses. Unfortunately for Tom the women only ever want his money or his coke; they simply use him. Fiona knows this and does not take any of his sluts, as she puts it, by their word. Fiona will go spare if she ever catches wind that Frankie Twirp is fucking with her firstborn, Tom Crane.

Then there was Barney who ran the Tavern, although Frank was never really into him again it was the alcohol and coke that kept her sneaking back there. Then there was Tyler Turner, her Will J's best pal. How she has sex with a young man her own son's age I will never know. Tyler Turner was a little wrong'un just like Will J but he had been helping Frankie sort money out for Will J.

Frankie had been driving Tyler to meet various rogues to get cash for Will J to put in numerous other criminals' bank accounts. One can only imagine what the hell is going on in the jails of today. Frankie had also been making some extra cash from selling her own depression tablets and any other medication she can get the doctor to prescribe her. From her Temazepam alone she can make an extra £50 cash a week and apparently sometimes she can make over £100 a week selling all of her prescriptions. She doesn't like to do this too often though as she leaves herself short of her medication. Not that she needs any of it, it really is just another free source to get her high. No wonder the NHS is in deficit. Tonight Frankie was out in Rochester with the young Tyler Turner himself. Both Frankie and Tyler were drinking in the Dickens Inn when a fight broke out between Frankie and a red-haired girl. It turns out the red-haired girl, known as Tilly Mills, was the same red-haired girl that had apparently been fucking William White for ten years and unfortunately for Frankie she is also friends with Frankie's young plaything Tyler Turner.

Frankie thought she had seen this young red-haired mouthy thing around before but couldn't quite put her finger on it. Tilly knew exactly who Frankie was and was cunningly judging the right moment to let Frankie know exactly who she was. Tilly was excited at the thought of exposing the fact she had been fucking Frankie's old man for the best part of 10 years. When Tyler went to the bar to get more drinks Tilly seized the opportunity.

'Frankie, isn't it? Erm I think I owe you an apology. Well in fact I don't think I do I know I do. You deserve the truth!'

Frank looked at the girl with a very confused face but said nothing.

'Well the thing is I have been having an affair with William for the best part of 10 years!' blurted Tilly.

Frank did no more than pick up her glass and smash it into Tilly's face. There was blood everywhere. Frank was saturated, her once white dress now looked pink. Tilly's mouth and nose were completely split open. Tilly was hysterical. There was security everywhere. Frankie stood silently staring in shock.

The police arrived within minutes. The blue sirens brought Frankie back to reality. Tyler spotted the carnage that had befallen Frankie and Tilly and as soon as he heard the sirens he made a run for it. Tyler mumbled under his breath,

'I can't afford to be wrapped around that shit, Frankie or no Frankie.'

Tilly was screaming at the police and pointing at Frankie. 'She attacked me!'

As the police homed in on Frankie one single lonely tear rolled down her cheek. Frankie could not believe her ears let alone her eyes. What had she done? William made her this way. Frankie knew in her heart of hearts that he, William, would most definitely be the death of her one of these days, one way or another William was responsible for her angry and reckless behaviour, the consequences of William's infidelities were to be the fall of Frankie.

Tilly was still screaming her mouth off as the police read Frankie her rights. 'You silly cunt Frankie he fucked me off a few months back, he got a new mort, some scrawny mousy-haired thing! Reckon it's serious you know he never ignored me in 10 fucking years! I'm as broken as you. I loved him too you know! Even had seven abortions for that man! And all I wanted was your help to find his new whore!'

Frankie could not fathom the shit this girl was coming out with. Frankie did not respond she just followed the police. The police knew Frankie all too well and did not even discuss whether or not her two youngest boys were being cared for. They had already sent a police car around to Frankie's home to check anyway.

John Boy answered the door and told the police to fuck off and then the poor innocent little mite only went and dropped the bombshell that no one was home. Poor lad, he knew no better. They do say we are the product of our parents! John Boy without even realising managed to give the police just the right amount of information that they needed to try and screw William and Frankie over. No normal parent would ever want their beloved children left in the hands of the law, and Frankie and William White for all that they are, would kill before social services got hold of their children. The police obviously called social services.

# Fifteen

Sadie was sound asleep, baby Kate was moaning and still Sadie slept through. I was just putting baby Kate's dummy back in when I noticed the flash of the blue lights outside that were illuminating the bedroom. Although there were no sirens, I knew that the excruciating brightness of the blinding blue lights belonged to that of a police car. I went over to the window and could now see that there were two police officers sitting outside in their car, their lights flashing away adding to the Christmas funfair of lights that were scattered pretty much over every house on the street. However there really was no need to add their blue presence to the already colourful charade of the street. Attention seeking blue bastards, I thought. It's Christmas fucking Eve!

I slowly crept out of my daughter's room and did no more than pop round to Frank's to check everything was ok. I knocked on the front door to be told by John Boy to,

'Fuck off you smelly arse pigs.'

I replied softly, 'John Boy, it's Kate mate, what's going on? Where's ya mum, mate?' John Boy opened the door as soon as he realised it was me. Although initially when John Boy thought it was the police knocking he was being mouthy, when he heard it was me and then when he saw me he started to cry.

'I dunno man, she went out ages ago. She does it every night, sometimes she's not even back in the mornings. Me and Josh get up and get our own breakfast! You know this anyway, Kate, we're always at yours.' John Boy was not his cocky wannabe big boy self and his spoken words and emotion only reinforced his childlike innocence. The poor boy was sobbing. The way he held his head in his hands in despair at his situation made my heart melt and get angry at his bullshit parents. What possessed some people?

I cuddled him and pointed towards the sofa and told John Boy to, 'Sit there for a minute.' I went out to speak with the two police officers. They were not very helpful. I politely said that Frank had asked me to keep an eye on them and asked what the problem was, hoping they would give me some information. Obviously the flashy controlling blue bastards didn't. I tried calling Frankie. There was no reply, just voicemail. I knew I would have to call William. William answered immediately. I was shocked. I definitely thought he would ignore my call. However I was not calling for myself it was for his boys. I didn't waste any time in explaining the situation to William and he arrived there within 10 minutes.

The police had to inform him of their call to social services. William advised them to call them back and let them know there had been a misunderstanding and that the children's father was now here. The police officers were so uncooperative. They were refusing to let William just take the children until the social workers arrived. This took three hours to resolve. The poor boys.

Well, to be honest, Josh slept through the whole drama. However poor little John Boy was in a right state, worried about his mother, worried the law was going to take him and his baby brother, he is only thirteen he shouldn't have to worry about this stuff, I thought.

All I kept saying was, 'For fuck's sake give the poor bloke a break!' meaning Will. The social worker was grilling him 'like he was some fucking paedophile,' as I liked to put it, which made me angry. 'He aint no fucking nonce love, seriously you need to go and fucking catch some real fucking nonces, you are barking up the wrong tree here!'

William touched my arm affectionately and said, 'Don't worry, Kate, she knows I'm no nonce she's just doing her job, and really we should be thanking her!' The social worker looked at William and smiled. God he was so fucking charming even the frumpy criss-cross checked stuck-up-her-own-arse social worker fell for him.

'If you could just give us your address Mr White then that way we can ensure that if anything like this occurs again and your neighbour isn't around to contact you we can send a police officer around to inform you of the unfortunate situation. Also I have to tell you I will be informing my superiors about tonight's events and I am sure you and the children's mother, Mrs White, is it, will have an appointment to attend to discuss future mutual parenting responsibilities so this kind of problem does not surface again.

You are aware Mr White that your children's mother is at present effectively out on bail and well, until this evening, she is now looking at another charge so you and your family's case, as you can understand, is a matter for further investigation.'

Both William and me sat in silence, shocked at this uptight martyr of a woman. The sarcasm that flowed naturally from her. I felt like she could see straight through mine and William's illicit love affair.

The social worker finally completed her assessment and eventually confirmed that it was safe enough for the boys to stay with their father. Although I had not seen William since that awful night with Tilly, I felt completely at ease around him. This was probably because whilst waiting for the frumpy, criss-cross social worker, William had had a chance to speak with me face to face and convince me that Tilly was just an easy plaything and that she was a liar and he hadn't known her for longer than five minutes. I, when in front of William, would believe anything he told me. I was totally mesmerised by the man. To me, he was like my own personal drug addiction, I craved him, thought about him far too much, and became a gullible weak feeble woman when I was around him.

Frank had now run out of electric so we really had no choice but to take the boys around to my house. Again, I gave up my bed for the boys. This was becoming a regular occurrence, I thought. It was now 5am, Christmas day morning. William, prior to the evening's events, was planning to fly off to Gran Canaria today. Frankie was being an absolute controlling cunt and refused point blank to let him have them for Christmas. William could not deal with the drama from Frank so he let her have her own way and just thought he'd fuck off for the week and in doing this he had nothing Christmassy in at his place and obviously everywhere was closed now so he couldn't even do a mad trolley dash if he tried. Therefore my offer of a bed on Christmas Eve was far too appealing for William White to consider refusing.

'There is a fucking god out there! I couldn't have conjured tonight up if I tried! A hot horny woman for crimbo! Never did I think this one up, Kate! But high fucking five, what a turn out!' William said this whilst he stared straight at me, his eyes boring into mine. I smiled an ambiguous smile and said nothing. Rather than dragging the boys and all their Christmas presents to his apartment where there was no tree and no food, William knew it made sense and he was over the moon that I had made such a thoughtful gesture. However I still felt very anxious about him and wondered where this would leave me if I allowed our affair to resume.

I dismissed his flirtatious jibes and said, 'I think you staying here is better for your sons actually Will, that way they won't feel too unsettled! Or worry about their mother! Then hopefully the boys in blue will let her out tomorrow so John Boy and baby Josh will get to see her on Christmas day at least.'

William laughed and responded warmly to me, 'Babe you got to be joking they won't be letting that silly cunt out til after Boxing Day! It's shut up shop bank holiday! Fucking irresponsible whore! Fuck her she aint given one thought to them kids up there! I could wring the div's neck to be honest Kate. What fucking mother fucks off out Christmas Eve? The mongy cunt shoulda just let me have em!'

I could understand why Will was so frustrated with Frankie, of all the times, Christmas Eve! 'Well hopefully this may well be a hard lesson learnt for Frank, sober and banged up over Christmas without her boys will hopefully give her the wake-up call she very much needs, Will!' I replied. All said and done, I still cared about Frank and hated seeing my friend being so destructive of late. At least the boys now knew that Frank was safe and ok, just banged up! Sadie and baby Kate slept through the whole sorry saga. I'm sure Sadie will have her penny's worth in the morning when she sees our guests. I knew that Sadie would be ok with the boys, Sadie actually felt really sorry for them. To be honest they had been round more often than not the last few months, what with Frankie keeping on leaving them and so Sadie had no choice but to sympathise with John Boy and Josh and the unfortunate little worlds that they had been subjected to. It was Christmas after all, which as we all know, is all about the children and making sure they are happy. Here we both were again, me and

William back at my kitchen table having a drink. After the night's events, I think it was needed.

I certainly was far too tired for anything else. Although in the back of my head I kept thinking I should not be drinking alcohol but after this evening's turnout and the fact I didn't want Will to put two and two together and work out my pregnancy predicament, I slowly nursed a vodka. However, William certainly did have energy for more than just a drink. He could not resist grabbing out at me and pulling me into him. I pathetically struggled to say in a very weak and unconvincing tone, 'We can't, Will.'

Will ignored my doleful plea and carried on with his wandering hands. He was wild for me. I was now standing or should I say, Will held me up against the lounge door and proceeded to slowly touch my genital area as he sneakily slipped a finger into my ever so delicate box, his affectionate kisses were slowly caressing my neck and then he was nibbling away at my tongue. My body had succumbed to the powers of William White once again. William was erotic and horny as hell and he couldn't resist me. I was now sat arched backwards over the arm of the sofa, my head resting on the large plump crimson cushions that lay behind me, my legs were spread wide and high whilst William was thrusting his hardness deep inside and groping at my very tender swollen breasts.

The Christmas tree lights were singing and dancing away and in effect mirror imaging my own internal live performance. Shit, in the midst of my personal catharsis, I hope he doesn't notice my enlarged breasts or my slightly protruding tummy. I tried my very best to ignore the predicament I had managed to find myself in. But I really needed to deal with it. I still hadn't even done a pregnancy test. But to be honest I didn't think there was any point, my body was telling me that I was most definitely pregnant. I knew I was probably at least three months gone.

William White was not a silly man. Of course he had noticed the small curvaceous changes to my body. After we had both orgasmed we laid naked, entangled in each other's arms and that's when William bluntly said,

'When's it due, Miss Andrews?'

I timidly lay wrapped within him and nervously replied, 'I don't know, Will.' William didn't even question if it was his baby.

He simply said, 'I will be here for you Kate no matter what you decide.' William knew I had been with no other man. Not just because he had been keeping a close eye on me but also because he knew I was a true woman and he knew I loved him. Hence my shutting down on him over Tilly. Crazy jealous creatures were women, thought William. William reassured me that Tilly was just an easy lay and that she would always come sniffing back and that he never has and never will love Tilly Mills.

'It's you and only you that I fucking love right now, Miss Andrews!' declared Will. He just said it, so naturally, so truly and so charmingly. I felt so shocked but also extremely happy and overwhelmed. I cuddled into William and said nothing, but my touch told him everything that he needed to know. I couldn't fall asleep. I lay silently and savoured this very long overdue loving moment and the love of my life. Santa certainly had my best interests at heart this year, I thought cheekily. For a moment, I actually forgot about all the secrets and all the carnage that lay ahead of us.

# Sixteen

Sadie had woken before baby Kate. It was 9am Christmas morning and this was baby Kate's first Christmas and Sadie had gone all out and spoilt her little dolly. The tree was oozing full of presents which were all for baby Kate. There were only a few that were labelled to others.

Sadie had already had her present off her mum, it was a twelve-week mixed martial arts course that she starts in the New Year. Sadie was overjoyed with her mother's gift - she had of course requested it. Her mother always got her what she wanted and more. Guaranteed Sadie's stocking would consist of; a Dove gift set, a Lindt selection pack, Christmas socks, Christmas PJs, knickers and bra-lets. For as long as Sadie could remember that's exactly what her mum had bought her as stocking fillers. And as predicted at the end of her bed hung her stocking.

She peeked inside just to see if her mum had spiced it up. Nope, exactly what Sadie expected. She was lovingly looking at her baby and was still in shock that she belonged to her. Luckily Sadie had never looked at her daughter and been reminded of her corrupt biological father and his shameful act. The deep voice that she could hear was coming from downstairs and made Sadie jump. Sadie did not recognise the voice however, she did hear and recognise her mum laughing. This sound of laughter from her mother was absolutely wonderful to hear, thought Sadie, as her mum had been so sad lately.

Although her mum would try and mask her sadness Sadie could feel that she was far from her usual go-getter self. Sadie had put her mother's blue state down to the fling she'd had at work with the married guy. Well not that she'd ever told Sadie he was married but she was not silly. Sadie completely disagreed with this situation her mum had got herself into but still she hated seeing her mum so depressed. So the fact Sadie heard her mum laughing made her feel cheerful too but also she couldn't help thinking, who on earth is sat laughing casually in our house on Christmas morning?

Sadie couldn't resist giving her baby an excited squeeze which in turn woke her daughter, Sadie's intention. Sadie started singing, 'Happy Christmas to ya, Happy Christmas!' as she picked baby Kate up to go and find out who their mystery guest was. However, as Sadie opened her bedroom door, she nearly tripped over, over Josh. Josh was sitting outside her bedroom door, eagerly waiting for her and baby Kate.

'Oh little man! Wow what are you doing here?' Sadie lovingly stroked the little boy's head and continued with, 'Where did you spring from?'

Josh looked up at her with his most endearing look and said, 'Bubba K crmis!'

Her mum was now erratically climbing the stairs and briefly told Sadie what had happened last night and that William was in the kitchen too. Sadie immediately froze. Not that her mother noticed. Sadie glared at William and grunted a 'morning' as she strode into the kitchen passed him and into the lounge towards the tree and the bundle of presents. Josh was squealing with joy and delight, which in turn, hyped baby Kate up and she too was squealing, which allowed the awkward moment felt by Sadie to be distracted.

William seemed so happy and alive too, all this love and happiness made Sadie question her mother and her so-called fling at work. Sadie could see between the pair of them that they had had sex last night. Jesus, did her mother think she was fucking stupid? However Sadie was not going to let her mother's shenanigans cloud her first Christmas with her daughter. Sadie was also thrilled as Jack was coming over for Christmas dinner, she had bought him some aftershave and a pair of new Nike air trainers. Sadie was dead excited to give them to him, more so because Jack never got presents.

Sadie, although she came from a single-parent family, had always been spoilt by her mother. Sadie had everything she could have ever wanted and her mum would clean and scrub all and sundry to ensure her daughter had the latest gadgets, clothes, clubs etc. Sadie had pretty much thought that's what all kids got. However since she met Jack she now knows that all kids do not get everything. Jack said his mother and father had never bought him a gift. Sadie found this impossible to believe. But it is true.

When Sadie went to Jack's for the first time they had nothing, not even a sofa. They had plastic chairs that were supposed to be white however, they were green from rotten moss and stained yellow from the nicotine. The walls were dark brown but looked grimy with what looked like tea and coffee stains splashed all over them, there was also what could be described as blood and faeces smeared on the walls too, it was the most grotesque place that she had ever seen. Basically the whole place was yellow and brown from nicotine stains. The carpet was threadbare and what was left was disgustingly sticky, like patches of black chewing gum trodden so deep it had kinda of formed a plastic residue. There were soiled sheets hanging from the windows blocking any natural light making the house even more dark and stuffy than it already was. There was an old dirty torn mattress that laid upon Jack's bare wood floor. This was his bed, bedding that looked like dog blankets and smelt like them too, even though his parents had no animals! There were a couple of empty deodorant bottles on the floor, a pair of jeans and maybe a couple of t-shirts draped over a dirty white plastic garden chair that sat in the corner of the room, that was it, Jack's bedroom. It was sad, baron and bare, thought Sadie.

Jack was travelling down with Sadie's nan and Sadie couldn't wait to surprise him with her very thoughtful gifts.

Sadie was lucky really, as if it wasn't for her mum giving her £30 a week pocket money she would never have been able to save the money for all the presents she had indulged in. To be honest, Sadie had been saving since September 1st, and she didn't smoke and drink anymore so she never really had anything else to spend her money on other than those that she'd grown to love. She thoroughly enjoyed spoiling baby Kate, and Jack certainly deserved a treat, he had at the very least managed to bring her out of her deep dark depressive rebellious state without any questions or demands, which really touched Sadie.

Christmas Day went so well it really was probably one of the best Christmas days she had had in years. William was great with Jack and even offered him a job at one of his mate's garages. Tom Crane's funnily enough. I never realised that Will owned 50% of Tom's garage until he had shared this with everyone over Christmas dinner. Will was never the showy off type. He was actually quite coy.

'I ave many a business Kate, I thought you knew that! To be honest with ya babe in total I got my fingers in eight other legitimate businesses!' Will said this so casually. Like who includes the word legitimate? Really he didn't even realise that comment only allows others to assume that he must have an illegitimate business too! I thought William White was just another drug dealer and that was it! However, the whole legitimate talk made me think, had he given all that other naughty shit up? Had he fuck or he would never have described his business ventures as legitimate!

I'd never seen myself with a drug dealer but funny enough I could actually see myself with William White, certainly after such a wonderful Christmas. The whole 'family' day we had all shared only made me love him more. My forbidden fruit had me yearning and defying my own desires far too often. I really needed to gain some perspective on the whole fucked up infidelity 'daddy to one' and 'daddy-to-be situation'. Maybe I needed to shut down to his illegitimate side? If only I could erase the fact he was Sadie's father! Yet again, I was in a quandary with myself. Still no Frankie.

## Seventeen

'Mum! Aunt Lane is on the phone!' shouted Sadie. I was just getting ready when William came up the stairs. Apparently he needed the toilet. Yeah, sure he did! Everyone else was downstairs. The boys and Jack were playing the PlayStation in the lounge. Sadie, the baby and Kate's mother were in the kitchen preparing dinner. Therefore William seized his opportunity to seduce me.

William locked the bathroom door and put the shower on. This unexpected entrance startled me. I was now clean, my hair had already been blow-dried, my face was now full of make-up, and there was no way I was getting back in that shower! For no one. Of course we were not taking a shower! And as I was still pretty much naked other than a cotton towel covering my modesty this only allowed William's task of seducing me that much easier.

William now had me bent over the bath, quietly thrusting away inside me and at the same time making sure not to arouse any attention or suspicion from any un-wanting ears and eyes. I was so wet! William only had to glide past and my knickers would be damp and for years this was all it was, just a flutter! And now here he was in my house, in my bathroom and deep inside both my body and mind.

How, I ask myself, had I finally got my dream of William White and his desire for me? Only me! How? Had he ever thought about me? And why now after all these years? The thing that really like really bugged me was that William had never queried Sadie's father! I would often mull this over and send myself insane with my own questions and theories. Surely any man would question the paternity of a child that could potentially be theirs! We were interrupted by our daughter. Sadie was screaming up the stairs.

'Mum. Phone. Mum, phone!'

I sneaked out of the bathroom and left Will to shower. 'I'm coming babe! Who is it?' I shouted to Sadie as I walked down the stairs.

'It's Auntie Lane,' responded Sadie whilst she was still chatting to Laney. Fuck, I've not spoken to her since her freaky lesbo act! Sadie handed the phone over.

'Hi darling, Merry Christmas, so sorry I've not called we've had a bit of drama here, I've not had a chance to think!' I said this to my friend in an awkward apologetic tone. Laney was absolutely fine.

'No worries, presh, guessed you got busy! And to be honest doll I was wasted yesterday, but I woke up this morning and thought I must come and see you all! I have presents and was going to drive over shortly!' Laney pretty much told me that she was coming over! There really wasn't that much of a 'can I?' or 'will you be home today for my visit?'

'Of course, mate, it will be lovely to see you,' I responded, emphasising the word 'mate'. However, inside I was cringing at the thought of seeing my best friend. But I carried on and asked Laney, 'Have you any plans for dinner today, mate?' Of course Laney didn't have plans other than the fact that she was coming here to see lucky old me! 'Oh stay and have some lunch with us, the more the merrier, Lane! And it is Boxing Day you can't eat alone.'

I was actually wanting to run. I knew this would be a circus but still the invite just flew out before I even had a chance to think of the potential dire consequences that Laney could cause today! What if Laney clocks the connection between me and Will? Or what if she decides to tell my whole family that I'm in denial and actually a lesbian? I winced at the thought. I was cringing that I hadn't spoken to Laney since that awful day back in the summer. Surely Lane will have a few drinks and play up. I was dreading the next few hours.

'Oh fuck, I haven't got her anything!' I frustratingly said to Sadie and Mum. I then proceeded to ask, 'Mum please don't be offended but you know the white musk gift set you got me from The Body Shop, do you mind if I give Laney that from the girls?'

Kate's mother replied in a sarcastic tone, 'Well fucking hell Kate, why you asking me? You normally give my presents back to me for Mother's Day!' All three ladies laughed at this. It was so true, I thought.

Laney arrived literally twenty minutes later, laden with gifts and champagne. All said and done Laney had been a fantastic godmother to Sadie, not just gift wise, she did genuinely care. I really hoped that we could move on from the whole love lesbian fantasy that Laney had become fixated on. Laney had plenty of boxes of chocolates and sweets that she gave to John Boy and Josh. She was a sweet, generous girl, shame she never had any children of her own. This would have grounded Laney. Still Laney slipped an extra one hundred pounds each to Sadie and Jack. They were elated to say the least. Sadie was spoilt. But I loved this and would never want it any other way. Laney left her gift for me until last. It was a small diamond encrusted box that looked far too intimate from just a girl-friend. I tried my best to look excited and not look too shock, shit, scared, surprised at her over-the-top gift!

'Oh, Mum look at the rock on that, ya so lucky!' screamed Sadie, eyes wide with excitement. I was shocked and very much embarrassed! The ring resembled that of a very extravagant engagement ring. All eyes were on me.

'Oh gosh I don't know what to say, Lane! This must have cost a small fortune!' I thanked my friend humbly and felt my face warm with discomfort from my friend's very generous gift. Laney stated that it was a friendship ring and tenderly kissed me full bam smack on the lips. I felt the rush of red stain my face. William had walked back into the kitchen right at that very awkward kiss moment. He was looking so fresh and his eyes were boring into me. With a confused face and an unknown grin he gave me a cheeky wink.

Sadie was far too busy admiring the eighteen-carat gold oversized diamond ring that Laney had bought me to notice William's wink. She was excitedly trying the ring on and too preoccupied to even notice my cheeks flush red, and Mum was far too excited about her new sewing machine that Laney had bought her to take a blind bit of notice about my uncomfortable discomfort and embarrassment at the whole situation. However Laney was staring straight at me with her eyes wide in an all-knowing state.

Then I looked at each and everyone in the room and it was like I had only just realised that I was hiding something, something big, from each and every single one of them. Mum was none the wiser to William being Sadie's father, well in fact none of them knew this! Then there was the fact William and me were having sex and I was pregnant! And Laney and her declaration of dedicated devotion of love for me! I couldn't have conjured the sorry stories up if I'd tried! Right now all Kate wanted to do was run and not stop!

Before I even had a chance to offer a sensible drink, Laney was pouring the champagne for everyone. I made my excuses that I hadn't eaten a single thing yet and I would be nursing a bad head if I considered a glass of bubbly right now. Laney was not convinced and ignored my silly pleas and insisted I have at least one glass.

'It's Christmas for fuck's sake, Kate! What the fuck happened to you? Anyone would think ya a fucking grey granny!' joked Laney.

'I am a granny just not a grey one!' I sarcastically responded. I drank the champagne. The last thing I needed right now was to raise any suspicions. Laney played right up. She got blinding drunk and kept trying to kiss William. It was really embarrassing at points. The audacity of Laney May Meeks still amazed me. Laney decided to give Will a lap dance/a striptease. Will was slightly drunk so he took Laney and her flirtatious ways in jest, she was now half-naked and asleep on the sofa. Personally, I thought that Laney's precarious promiscuous act was for my benefit. I could not tell if Laney had noticed anything between me and Will.

Will took the boys back to his apartment. We thought this would be best not just because of the lack of room at my house but also because at least when Frankie turns up she won't see a happy family environment and give her somewhat already wayward mind something else to consider. I changed my bed and couldn't wait for sleep to coma my mad mind. I had all sorts running on in my head. What will I tell Sadie about me, William and the unexpected baby? What will I tell Frankie? Will I tell Sadie and William that they are, in fact, father and daughter? How did it all come to this?

# Eighteen

I woke to a mad crazy Fiona banging my door down. 'Kate, Kate, open the door I need to speak to you now!' screamed Fi-Fi through the letter box.

Sadie was now hanging out the window shouting, 'Nice one Fi, you've only gone and woke the baby!'

'Sorry my babe, but I really need to talk with your mum! It's urgent!' responded Fiona apologetically.

I was at the door. 'Morning Fi!' I tried to sound cheery. Fiona went off on a mad rage. Basically Tom had told Fiona about his relationship with Frankie. Fiona had spent Christmas with Tom at his caravan over at Allhallows. Poor Tom was devastated he found out Frankie was still fucking Barney. Apparently Tom has fallen for Frankie. Fiona said he got blinding drunk last night and told his mother everything that's been going on between him and Frankie the last few months. Fiona was fuming.

'Where is the little fuckin whore? Did you know, Kate?' Fiona raged.

I said I'd had heard through the grapevine but didn't know for sure. Frankie never told me. I had seen both Frankie and Tom a couple of times late at night out the back. I did not want to get involved in street gossip hence I didn't repeat what I had seen to anyone.

Fiona seemed to calm a little once I had told her about the most recent events with Frankie Twirp. Even Fiona had a heart and knew Frankie had a messed up childhood so she could at least sympathise with Frank's rotten roots. However Fiona won't have anyone mug her boy off as she put it.

'What the fuck was Frankie thinking? Is Will going to let her have the kids back, babe?' asked Fiona.

'To be totally honest with you Fi, I genuinely don't know, we didn't discuss that, we just tried to make the boys' Christmas the best it could be considering the diabolical circumstances,' I answered flatly.

Laney's voice was heard before we could even see her. 'Morning my fellow campers.' In walked Laney, full of life.

I looked at Laney and asked in amazement, 'How do you do it?'

Laney completely dismissed my question and cheerfully shouted, 'Merry Christmas beautiful bootylicious Fiona!'

'Merry Christmas lovely lady,' replied Fiona whilst Laney was bending down to give her a Christmas kiss. Then Laney looked straight at me and mouthed,

'What?'

I couldn't help but laugh at her, she was so coy. 'You, you were so drunk last night you ended up strip teasing for William in front of everyone!' I said this in a high pitched tone. 'Oh chillax, Katieee, it's Christmas! I think it's another day for a Christmas Champers brekky! You want one Fiona? We know you won't ya boring bugger over there!' squalled

Laney whilst looking at me with an unpredictable gaze. Much to my dismay Laney was stood in my kitchen in just her knickers and a vest top pouring the champagne into coffee cups! Like this was a normal everyday occurrence!

'Really, do you have to? At least get some glasses, Lane!' I said with a pang of annoyance. Laney ignored me and carried on chatting to Fiona about how she thinks I might just fancy William.

'You always said he was a drug-dealing wrong'un a Kate! You both looked pretty cosy to me!' Laney knew exactly what she was insinuating; her tone oozed sarcasm. I turned scarlet. Both Laney and Fiona were now looking at me for some sort of response, denial at least. I was saved as Sadie walked into the kitchen with baby Kate, so all the attention was now focused on the baby. I felt a sense of relief. The last thing I needed was any talk of me and William getting out. However, I was certain Laney knew exactly what was going on between me and William. Whether she would expose me is another story. I never thought Laney would ever be the one to stab me in the back. But what with Laney declaring her undying love for me recently I wasn't so sure of my friend. Jealousy did all sorts to a person, and I would not be so confident of my friend's loyalty anymore. Laney was already half-drunk, she hadn't even eaten this morning. Sadie even looked annoyed by Laney's loud, drunken manner. I noticed this as Sadie would not let Laney hold baby Kate. Laney was swaying and trying to make baby Kate give her a cuddle, however, the baby was happy playing in her ball pit.

Sadie eventually snapped at Laney, 'Leave off, Lane, she don't want to be pulled about she's not a doll!' I think Laney was extremely embarrassed by Sadie's remark as she quickly responded an awkward,

'Sorry!' and quipped that she was going to get herself clean.

'There's plenty of hot water, you'll feel better after a shower, Lane.' I felt my friend's embarrassment and tried to disguise this by talking about the hot water. I didn't know if Laney was being sarcastic. Clean in alcohol or clean from a shower? From Laney's tone, I  most definitely thought Laney was being sarcastic and in fact I wasn't so sure that Laney was happy being this intoxicated of late. Maybe I should try and talk with her at some point, at least try and clear the air and hopefully I will get my friend back.

Fiona seemed a little relaxed after her glass of bubbly and went next door for a lie down. Sadie was banging on about the pantomime at The Brooke Theatre and that she had booked the two o'clock showing and wish she had booked the four o'clock as it is now twelve and she had still not sorted her and the baby out.

'Chill Sade, I will watch the baby and get her washed and dressed whilst you go get yourself showered and clean, you got a good hour and a half before you need to leave. Go get clean and you'll feel brand new, my little darling! Oh and Sadie can you please give Laney a break she is obviously going through some shit?' I spoke affectionately.

'Thanks, Mum, that helps! But really, are you sure about Lane, she is so annoying me with her drinking! It's like she's stuck on repeat!' Sadie chuckled. 'Don't worry I'll be nice!' Sadie responded to her mother.

Sadie did not need to be told twice. She was off up the stairs to go and make herself look pretty and check on her surrogate aunt. Whilst Sadie, Jack and baby Kate were at the theatre this would give me the perfect opportunity to speak with Laney, alone.

Bang, bang, bang. There was clearly someone at the door. I thought it sounded like a police knock. It was Frankie.

'Oh Kate, where's my boys? What a mad mash up, oh I'm such a cunt, me babies' Christmas! Where are they, Kate? Please don't tell me that social services have them! Oh it's making me sick! Them bastard's aint told me fuck all in there, treated me like a fucking animal the whole of fucking Christmas!' Frank didn't come up for air. I was trying to calm her down. But Frank was a rambling mess. I reassured her the children were safe and that they were with William. Frank said she had been calling Will for the last hour as soon as she had been released and he was not answering. Frank looked absolutely bedraggled. I suggested that Frank should go home get herself cleaned up, which will make her feel better, and she will see things in a clearer perspective and then hopefully Will should have contacted her by then.

I actually thought to myself, for fuck's sake this is the third person I have told to go get clean and they will feel better. Like a shower that automatically washes the dirt from your skin and in some crazy delusional thought the shower can also wash the sins away at the same time. I knew this was a load of crap, however, I felt it was an appropriate gesture in all three cases.

I looked Frankie up and down and her clothes that she still wore were covered in blood. You would have thought that the boys in blue would have at least given her a change of clothes. Apparently, she has been charged with grievous bodily harm. Frank said she pleaded guilty as there were too many witnesses. Frank also said that her duty solicitor advised that if she cooperated and basically pleaded guilty that the Crown Prosecution Service would take this into consideration when they came to sentencing her. However, the solicitor also told Frankie that she was looking at a high chance of getting a prison sentence. As Frank had had previous violent arrests in the past this did not go in her favour. The fear oozed from Frankie. I had never seen Frank so scared and knew that if they ended up sending her down that Frank may never come back from that. The fact she is so close to losing her boys, Frank knew she had to make some big changes to her life in order to keep them. The thought of her boys going into care or worse to her mother was enough for Frankie to want to take them all and jump off the Rochester Bridge.

As much as William was a doting father she really couldn't see him stepping up, his businesses always came first. Frank did ask herself how the fuck she could love a man who thinks of money and drugs before his blood? Then again her own mother was cut from the same cloth so why this shocked Frankie she'll never know! Maybe it's a pattern of behaviour that Frankie had become accustomed to – for her whole life she had never been put first. Frank knew she had been far too destructive of late and for the sake of her boys she must take control. Just as Frank was walking out the front door she paused and looked at me and said,

'Oh yeah Kate, the little carrot whore only reckons Will has dumped her and got a new little number!' Frankie's eyes were wide with inquisitiveness. 'I can't help meself, the curiosity has been nagging away at me! Who the fuck is she, Kate? Why does this little ginger gymslip think she knows my old man better than me?' I felt myself blush. Frank did not seem to notice my flushed cheeks. Thank God.

I responded in a I don't know anything tone. 'Frank don't go getting yourself wound up babe, this girl's probably just shouting her mouth off about nothing!' Frank didn't look convinced. As I was seeing Frank out I could also see Fiona in my garden and thought, fuck girl you only got yourself another earache to come now!

I shut the door quickly and went straight to the kitchen and wacked up the radio to drown out any commotion coming from outside. I just did not need any more drama in my world right now. I had managed to wash and dress baby Kate whilst counselling Frank and now the dear little pink bundle was sleeping peacefully in her bouncy chair. Laney came into the kitchen and strode past me, and just a bit too close for comfort. Laney brushed past my breasts as she went by and remarked,

'You had a secret tit job, Kate? Your breasts are bigger!'

I felt very uncomfortable but replied with a smile. 'Of course not you silly mare, like I can afford new tits!'

Laney looked at me with suspicious wide eyes and made a distrustful sound. 'Mmm!'

I looked at my friend and assertively said, 'I didn't want to do this whilst Sadie was home, but you seem to give me no fucking choice! Now look Laney you have been my fucking friend forever and I have never failed you as a friend. I cannot help that I do not have any intimate feelings for you at all! I do not want to lose you as a friend, however, I am not prepared to put up with your drunken flirtatious insulting behaviour any longer!'

Laney knew I was serious. Laney seemed to be digesting what I had just said to her and then lovingly responded. 'I love you Kate always have, always will! And I really don't want to upset you I just can't seem to help myself! And I know you're fucking Will, I could see it as soon as I walked in yesterday! It broke me Kate. I can tell you love him!' There were now tears falling from Laney's eyes.

I cuddled her and said, 'Look Lane I can't help my feelings and it's all such a mess! I don't know whether I'm coming or going! And the last thing I need is you going all jar pot crazy on me!'

Laney looked up at me and said, 'Well fancy getting involved with William Fucking White! You're asking for trouble, Kate! What about poor Frank? Your so-called mate?'

'Alright Lane, fuck me I know, I feel an absolute cunt! But fuck, I never planned this, any of this!' I responded in defence.

'Well, my dear friend, you are not going to be able to hide your bump and breasts much longer!' Laney said as a matter of fact.

I looked down at my very voluptuous figure and knew I had to think of something to get away from this mess I had got myself into. Sadie and Jack were bouncing down the stairs so, therefore, mine and Laney's conversation temporarily came to a halt.

# Nineteen

New Year came and went rather peacefully compared to Christmas. It was mid-January and I had now been to see the doctor and was on my way to my first scan. It certainly was a beautiful bright sunny winter's day. The clear blue skies and the warmth of the sun beating down on my face made me feel positive about my new-fangled journey that I was about to embark on.

I was fourteen weeks pregnant. William was aware of the scan, however, he didn't show up. Apparently he got caught up with business.

I tried to understand William's demanding businesses but felt little faith and much disappointment when it came to William. In fact, I sensed all men were pretty unreliable and unpredictable creatures, love or no love. William apologised profusely of course and promised he would take me for dinner that evening. At least I wouldn't have to lie to Sadie where I was going. I had managed to tell Sadie about me and William. Sadie had pretty much guessed anyway and I certainly did not want to deny my daughter's perception and cause more distrust. Sadie was ok, to my surprise. Sadie had seen my happiness and explained that if she hadn't witnessed such a love she wouldn't have been so accepting of her and William's love affair. However, I hadn't quite had the courage to tell Sadie about my own pregnancy. I told myself as soon as I worked out what I was going to do, I would tell my daughter about her new brother or sister-to-be. I knew that we would have to move, not just because of space but living next door to Frankie was not a good plan, given the current circumstances.

William had said me and the children could move in with him. However, I knew that would be far too much far too soon, not for me but for Sadie. Therefore that offer was out of the question, only for now anyway, I had told William.

I was slightly nervous. I hadn't seen William for a couple of weeks. Although we spoke daily, Will was just always too busy or it was just simply due to the awkward situation that we were in. It wasn't the easiest task trying to snatch a few hours here and there with William. Certainly when Frank turned up at mine ten thousand times a day. The conversations would be completely focused on William and how Frankie will never let him go. This was becoming a big problem for me, what with the guilt I felt anyway. It was daily torture seeing Frankie and listening to her heartache.

William had let Frankie have the boys back after a few days of making her sweat. However, if Frankie gets a prison sentence William will have to have the boys full-time. I knew that this would be complicated for her and William, hence this was another reason I was not prepared to move in with William. I knew if I was ever going to be able to move forward with my new life I would have to move a little further out. At least a motorway journey away. Frank doesn't like to drive on motorways, so for me this was a bonus right now. I knew that I would have to eventually move out of the Medway towns in order to find contentment. Given Frankie's phobia of motorway driving I believed Frankie wouldn't follow me and give me any grief. However, as quick as I felt relief from this freedom of thought I was all too aware that Frankie could easily get someone else to drive her, revenge as such.

I found myself looking at private lets. I always vowed I would never give up the security of our council home. Yet here I was scouring the internet for a new non-council home. I felt I had no choice but in order for me to survive this mess that I had found myself in, I had to move away from my home. I was very aware of time and knew I had to act fast. There were two beautiful large three-bedroomed houses that stood out for me. However, they were both in Herne Bay, a seaside resort in Kent. It seemed the rent was cheaper down that way, but despite the fact the rent was still cheaper I still couldn't afford it. There was no way I could get two thousand pounds together for the deposit. And I would never ask William for the money, I was far too proud. The problem was I didn't know a single soul with that sort of money. Well there was one person that had that kind of money, Laney. I arranged a viewing of each property, knowing that I had no other alternative than to ask Laney to lend me the deposit.

'Kate, you can do this,' I said out loud to myself. I knew Laney well enough to know she would help me, even though Laney was hurt with me for not engaging in her lesbian fantasy. I trust my friend will still be there for me.

# Twenty

Sadie had just finished school. It was a Friday and the first week back after Christmas. It had been the longest and coldest week for Sadie. Finding out about her mum and William's relationship had not helped Sadie's mood.

Sadie seemed to be very edgy and agitated by her mum wanting to be with William White. Although Sadie tried her hardest to ignore the White family, this was extremely tough when they were being shoved down her throat. Sadie, at points, thought she would physically vomit over all of them. But Sadie could see how happy her mother was, so, unwaveringly, Sadie attempted to close her eyes to her mother and William White's relationship.

Sadie has, however, recognised her own destructive behaviour and this anger has only risen again since her mother told her about her illicit relations with the ill-disciplined Mr White. She had fallen out with Jack this week and she had also fallen out with one of her closest friends, Molly Cross. Sadie had grown up with Molly, they had started pre-school together and were the very best of friends. Molly was very much like Sadie; they were often mistaken for sisters, which they both revelled in. Molly became a little distant with Sadie when baby Kate was born, this was because Molly could not understand why her friend had to be so secretive about baby Kate's father. Molly had seemed to have dropped the whole 'who's the daddy?' subject for a while but as soon as they returned to school after the Christmas holidays Molly did not shut up about baby Kate's father and his hidden identity. Sadie eventually snapped at Molly that morning whilst they were on break in the canteen and now Sadie was feeling really crap and emotional.

Sadie looked up at the skies and they were as grey as her mood, she cuddled into herself to try and find some grace from the ever so sharp wind that she was up against right now. It wasn't a long walk home, maybe fifteen minutes maximum, but today for Sadie it felt like hours to get home. As soon as Sadie walked in the front door and saw her mum she burst into tears.

I immediately went straight over to embrace and comfort my emotionally crushed daughter.

'Whatever is the matter, Sade?' I asked. Sadie proceeded to sob. I felt helpless. 'Please, darling tell Mum what is it, why are you so upset?' I pleaded with my daughter but still it was just heart-wrenching sobs that bellowed from Sadie. 'It's your birthday tomorrow darling, I've arranged something super special for us!' I hoped maybe if I changed the subject Sadie may calm down. However, it seemed no matter what I said, Sadie was distraught and was not letting on what had happened to cause her so much suffering and distress. Baby Kate was happily watching *Shrek* and thank God she didn't seem fazed by her mother's emotional breakdown, I thought, as I stroked my granddaughter's cheek whilst gently sitting Sadie on the sofa.

'Is it Jack, baby girl, have you two still not made up?' I was soft when I asked my daughter.

Sadie immediately responded, 'No, Mum, it's really not Jack!' Jack had been calling Sadie all week but Sadie just couldn't face him. Jack hadn't actually done anything wrong. Sadie just shut down on him. Sadie herself didn't even really know why so she certainly couldn't explain to her mum why she'd been ignoring Jack.

'You've had a tough year darling, maybe it's best if you just focus on baby Kate and your studies,' I advised my daughter. Sadie silently agreed, with a slight nod of her head. 'A nice hot bath will make you feel brand new, baby girl,' I told my daughter knowing full well that a bath may soothe her for now but it certainly wouldn't mend whatever it is that seems to have shattered her.

'If only a bath would heal my Sadie,' I was speaking on the phone to Laney, stressing my worries to my friend. 'What can be so bad, Lane? I wish she would just tell us who he is! She knows I won't judge her, for fuck's sake I haven't yet! I've only ever been there for her and the baby!' I was unaware Sadie was at the bottom of the stairs and could hear my whole conversation. Then out of nowhere Sadie appeared.

'Oh poor fucking Kate, her baby won't confide in her! It's not all about you, Mother! And I swear down on my fucking life may I drop down dead right fucking now, no more fucking talk of my baby's fucking shit cunt of a father! I promise you I will take my baby and fuck off and you will never see either of us again!' Sadie was wild with venom screaming at her mother. I awkwardly said to Laney I would call her back. Sadie was off back upstairs before I had even hung the phone up. Although I was beside myself with worry for my daughter I respected Sadie enough to honour her demands. My only problem with ignoring the identity of my granddaughter's father was that I was one hundred percent sure that he was my daughter's biggest delinquent.

I knew all too well in order for my daughter to deal with her demons over her baby's dad she has to face it head on and not bury it. I asked myself, how the fuck do I deal with this?

'God if Sadie hasn't even told her best friend she must be super ashamed!' I was chatting to my mum on the phone now, worried for my daughter. Sadie was sound asleep with baby Kate so I knew I was safe to talk the delicate talk. My mum was a practical lady and told me not to dwell. My mum was more interested in my situation than her granddaughter's right now. I accidentally told Mum everything about me and William. She was not best pleased. She insinuated I was far too old to be having another baby let alone with my mate's bloke. I came off the telephone feeling dreadful. I had telephoned my mother for advice on my own daughter, at which she was useless, and instead got a whole lot of mockery for my own foolish behaviours. I didn't intend to tell Mum about my shenanigans with William but it just came out. I suspect it was my hormones as I was an absolute emotional mess at the moment. William hadn't bothered calling me for several days. He completely blew me and the scan out, which only made me feel dreadfully lonely and so much worse about my erratic circumstances.

Sadie was awake at 3am. She was so restless and was irritated with herself for thinking about the night baby Kate was conceived. The thoughts angered and frustrated Sadie even more than ever before. Sadie thought that it would get easier but she now sensed that it will only get harder, especially now her mother was fucking William White.

Sadie lay silently, realising it is actually her fourteenth birthday today and it had been a hell of a journey since that degrading and shameful incident. Sadie hated herself right now. Sadie's phone started bleeping. It was Jack. Sadie couldn't deal with Jack either, he has been great with Sadie about the whole sex thing. The thing is Sadie won't engage in any sexual relations with Jack. The fear Sadie feels about ever having sex again is sending her into further despair. Jack is far from pressurising her but Sadie knows as a girlfriend of nearly six months she should be putting out. Sadie has decided to let Jack be free to find a girlfriend who can pleasure him because Sadie believes this will never be her. However Jack's persistence is starting to wear away at Sadie. In fact Sadie really misses Jack.

# Twenty-One

The journey was long, and the more I drove the more I cried. The tears they just kept on rising and falling. The pain of a broken heart was causing me to literally break down and with each sorry sob the tears were cascading and crashing against my very flushed cheeks. The discomfort was so intensifying it rose from the pit of my stomach to my heart and then into my conscious being. I knew I had lost control.

I drove to Laney's in hope of a shoulder to cry on and arrived in an absolute flood of tears as much as I tried to console myself I just couldn't manage it. I was supposed to be at work but there was no way I would have ever got anything done. Therefore I did no more than telephone my boss at quarter to five this morning and make some bullshit up that I had been being sick all night, ironic considering my situation. The confusion of my world and where to turn was all just far too overwhelming and I knew I had to find it in myself to gain some strength to confront the shit that I had caused.

'Oh I feel so bad I've phoned in sick! Fuck my boss! Why should I feel guilty? He didn't even give me a Christmas fucking cleaning bonus! But then I really can't afford to lose those cleans, Lane! Oh what have I gone and got myself into?' I was a complete mess! Crying and justifying my pretend sickness to Laney.

Laney shouted at me. 'Leave it out, Kate, who gives a fuck about some capitalist cunt! You got more important cunts to worry about!' Laney was clearly indicating William and Frankie were my more worrying cunts. I hated that Laney called William a cunt however, at the same time I felt like a pathetic cunt for even allowing myself to be protective of William.

William had gone quiet on me and I knew this was half the reason behind me being so emotionally distraught and actually had nothing whatsoever to do with my fragile hormones. I liked to think that William could stay faithful, however, I also was very aware that William White was a womaniser, he had always been a womaniser and would probably always be a womaniser. I sensed my love alone just didn't seem enough for William.

Laney appeared sober, which I was a little pleased about. Laney was even making coffee, something I hadn't seen for a long time. I seemed to be calming down. The cool, calm, hippy environment certainly helped me find a little composure. Laney's house was most people's dream home. An oversized iconic building with its ancient rustic features but modernised to a five-star standard; it really was a home to be proud of. There were joss sticks burning in every cubby hole making the place seem hazy. Laney May Meeks was a lucky girl. My envy at my friend was felt every time I entered Laney's wishful world. Laney was speaking to me in a very low tone.

'Look darling you just need to set yourself a little small target a day! It will all fall into place and you know I will be here for you every step of the way.'

I muffled, 'I was going to ask you if you could lend me a deposit to move away. I know I need to get away to gain some sort of perspective Lane on my situation and I do need your help!'

Laney didn't even question her friend's request. She literally said a simple, 'Yes of course.' Laney's kindness sent me into another emotional meltdown. Laney cuddled me and tried to reassure me that everything will be ok in the end. Laney also suggested that me and the girls were more than welcome to come and stay with her. It's not like she doesn't have the room. Laney went on to say, 'And don't you worry about the school run for Sade. I will do it! Anyways I am on a stay sober mission now and I think the school run will definitely help me, you know, be responsible and all that!' Laney said this with a laugh.

I was in too much of a state to make a decision. However, I was supposed to be viewing the two houses I had found in Herne Bay this afternoon, but knew that I wasn't going anywhere. The thought of having a little extra support really appealed to me right now. I knew that Sadie would be more than happy with their potential new living arrangement. Sadie loved Laney's place. And after last night's emotional breakdown, maybe a change of scenery will actually do Sadie some good.

A few hours later, I woke startled. I appeared to be in one of Laney's spare rooms. The winter sun was so strong seeping through the beautifully crafted sash windows that donned this manor. There were no curtains or nets hanging, they were like bare frames against unadorned walls. Cold cream marble tiles that wore a scatter of those dark red, purple and orange stripy flat mats echoed throughout this antique old house. They gave the place a bit of a colourful hippy flare. A complete contrast to my hand-me-down world. The complicated layers I had to deal with were all waiting for me at home and right now I could do with a less cluttered environment. I laid there in my temporary sanctuary and thought that I really did have the opportunity to make this my very own permanent refuge. There was silence throughout. A complete stillness. Not even a cackle from the heating. Where was Laney?

'Lane, Laney!' I shouted as I came down the swirling stairs. Nothing. I was standing in Laney's ever so oversized kitchen looking puzzled. Then I spotted a note stuck on the fridge with a silver magnet displaying the words NOTES. The note read: *Kate had to go to my alcohols meet. I'll see you or call you when I get back. Lane X.*

I felt fluffy and a bit confused. In a sense it was like I had been drinking alcohol but obviously I hadn't had a drop. I heard the clock chime! Still dazed I was faffing around looking for my phone to check the time!

'Fuck it's nearly three o'clock! Fuck! Fuck!' I now went into a flutter as I knew I had to make my way back for the girls in like 15 minutes and when on a good run it takes at least 30 minutes. I flew out the door and knew I was about to break every speeding law going! All the while wondering how the hell I ended up tucked up in Laney's spare bedroom. Since when did memory loss become a pregnancy symptom?

# Twenty-Two

Laney was at her Alcoholics Anonymous meeting and to her utter surprise she actually thought that these shitty lonely gatherings might just be helping her. The fact she could open up to these abused, alcohol-addicted strangers and not be judged for some of her less desirable acts, felt absolutely fucking liberating.

The first meet was pretty much, 'MY NAME IS ... AND I'M AN ALCOHOLIC. BLAH. BLAH. BLAH.' The second meet was a little more indulgent. The more she heard from those sorry arseholes only made her, Laney fucking May Meeks, feel alright about her own fuck ups. Yes, she had a first-class childhood. The perfect parents some might say. Then all of a sudden at the ripe age of sixteen her parents tragically died in a car crash. She was sent to live with her great aunt who lived in St Mary Hoo, a small village just past Rochester.

Laney lived a lonely existence for a while. But her new life soon then became an adventure. Laney filled her days with balmy country walks and scrumping fruit in the nearby farmer's fields. It was on one of those walks that she met the first woman she ever found sexually attractive. Laney excitedly told her alcoholic randoms about her most suppressed secret. Although she had been with boys - or should she say she'd had plenty of experience with those young gross smelly pubescent delinquents - it wasn't until she met the lovely Margo that she realised the repressed sexual desire that she held for women.

Margo was married to Geoffrey and they had a baby boy who was also called Geoffrey. The baby was probably around two at the time when Laney first met Margo. Margo was the most petite woman she had ever encountered, teeny tiny and very out there, in the sense she was wild, kind of eccentric with her views and held a very politically opinionated manner. A natural blonde lady, not the most womanly of women, a teenage boy figure however, Margo's personality certainly made up for what Margot lost in size.

Geoffrey was a banker and was always at work. He worked in the city and only ventured home at weekends. They had the most homely of homes. A small country cottage with a perfect white picket fence. Window boxes filled with lobelia and petunia. The contrast between the bright pink petunia and the subtle pale blue lobelia complemented each other and allowed the striking flowers to dominate the small cottage. They lived at the very back of Laney's aunt's land, at least two miles away from her aunt's house. Yet they moved away many years ago, no doubt because of Laney.

It was today here at her alcoholics' meet that she found herself disclosing this secret which she had carried for pretty much her whole adult life, why? She does not know! Or was she secretly ashamed? Margot also introduced her to recreational pills, ecstasy was the proper name that was used for the illegal tablets. The first time she encountered Margot she was crying. She was sat upon a wrought iron bench that was perched perfectly in the centre of her garden.

Laney walked past one summer morning and could hear the sad sobs coming from the wispy little woman that had befallen on her before she'd even had the chance to lay her eyes on her. Well, her being the nosy person she is, she could not help but ask if she were ok.

At first Margot ignored her, well at least she thought she was. Yet she still pushed for a response. Laney found herself walking down the garden path towards her and to her utter surprise Margot jumped up shouting at her, 'Get out, get out, get the fuck out!' Obviously, she turned right back around and thought sod you! You crazy lady.

She'd continued on with her casual normal predictable nature walk thinking what on earth could have happened to this poor soul for her to be so sad. The thing is although Laney's parents had tragically died she could not cry, even when she tried. Sometimes she thought she must be one of those emotionally retarded people that show no fucking emotion whatsoever. Now, she thinks it was most definitely a sign of post-traumatic stress disorder! What teenager doesn't shed a tear when unfortunately and unexpectedly is left orphaned so young? And in what was described as one of the most tragic circumstances some had seen?

It must have been a couple of hours later when Laney bumped into the crazy lady again, but she didn't seem so crazy this time. Margot was walking and pushing her baby in a stroller. Margot spotted me and immediately sped up her pace. At first she thought, oh gosh that mad woman is coming for me, and she was coming for her, but to apologise for her being so rude earlier. Apparently her baby had had her awake all night and she was feeling tired and emotional.

Margo invited Laney back to her cottage for a lemonade and she politely accepted her kind offer. It was when they went back for the lemonade that Margo told her how dreadfully lonely she had become since having baby Geoffrey.

'Oh Laney you sweet girl!' Margot had said. 'Let me give you some advice, enjoy your life at every opportunity as you never know when it will change and one day you may just end up stuck in a lonely marriage being a slave to everyone but yourself! Life was once an exciting adventure and now I feel it's more like a restricted lonely existence. It's like I have been bound up Laney! Oh gosh listen to me getting all deep on you! You beautiful girl you really are quite exquisite Laney!'

It was maybe not the exact speech Margo had delivered, but this was a close version and after Margot's philosophical advice she stroked Laney's cheek endearingly. It was then in that stroking moment that Laney felt her first flutter in her vagina. She had never felt a flutter of any kind even though she had already experimented with boys and sex by this age.

Life had become extremely lonely for Margot. At the age of thirty-six, with a baby and a husband that worked away in London all week and only came home at weekends, it was a far cry from her old life. The fact was Margo had always had a high flying career, as she too used to work in London with Geoffrey at a big high street bank and it now appeared that away from the glitz and the glam of London that poor Margo is battling against her new, lonely life as a mother. Margot and Geoffrey had lived a very hectic social existence prior to having baby Geoffrey and if they weren't attending charity events they would be at meetings, therefore late night restaurant dinners became the norm.

Margot felt her life was mundane and dull and was evidently yearning for some excitement. Once upon a time they lived for festivals and concerts. She used to work a sixty-plus hour week so there was never much time for alone thoughts, which it would seem this is what Margot was struggling to adapt to as well.

The cool evening was creeping in and Margot had put baby Geoffrey up to bed. She and Laney ate in the small kitchen. Margot had baked some potatoes which they had with cheese and coleslaw. It was the first time Laney had eaten that cheese and coleslaw mix with a baked potato, it was delicious. A simple meal and yet still one of her favourites to this day and she always thought of Margot when she ate it.

It was after supper that Margot offered Laney a little white wine spritzer. After their second glass Margot jumped up from her floral oversized armchair, well it probably wasn't an oversized armchair but in the small space of her cottage and the teeny tiny creature that sat upon the armchair only made the eccentric piece look enormous. Margot went to a little cream pot that was sitting on top of the decrepit wooden fireplace, which actually looked like it may have housed proper fire at some point, as black stains etched deep within its grain. Margot then came and sat back down next to Laney on her other oversized floral armchair, to be honest it wasn't even a squeeze considering two women were now sitting on one armchair. Margot then looked at Laney and said, 'We should have some fun Miss Meeks! Look what I have here!' She was holding her hand out to me which held around eight or ten blue pills.

Laney looked back at Margot and innocently asked, 'Is this heroin?' Margot looked at her laughing and replied, 'No dear Laney not heroin but they are recreational drugs called Ecstasy! Geoffrey and I would eat them like smarties at festivals! We had the most amazing experiences. You should try one with me, we will only do one each! Nothing too intense!'

With that Margot was putting one blue pill into my hand. 'We will do them together,' she told her. Laney did as she was told. At first nothing seemed to be happening. Laney still just felt fuzzy from the wine. Then out of nowhere she felt this euphoric feeling buzz through her veins into the dark depths of her body. Margot was laid back with her bare legs sprawled all over her.

Laney could vividly remember her whole body was slighting perspiring which made her feel very clammy certainly when Margot was rubbing her leg up against her hypersensitive skin.

It was then that Margot looked up at Laney and whispered, 'Let me taste you Laney?'

Laney couldn't respond, her body felt bolted to the floral wilderness surrounding her. She felt she was sinking into a deep filled bloomy softness. It was then she felt Margot's hand softly stroking her toned thighs. She was close enough to Laney's private parts for her to feel the thumping within her own tight little young pussy. No boy had ever evoked such a sense. The boys she had encountered at such a fresh age were clueless, rough, inexperienced fumblers. It was then I enjoyed my very first experience of another woman relishing the taste of her ripened cherry. Although this was Laney's first encounter of realising that she was in fact a lesbian, this out of body experience that she had endured with the ever so hot yummy mummy Mrs Geoffrey Margo Zackery, was also her first-ever experience of deep passionate love.

The love affair she shared with Margo continued until she was twenty-one. They had five long, secret ecstasy lesbian-fuelled sexual satisfactions. Then on one winter's Monday morning Laney drove as fast as she could to Margo's cottage, as she normally did on a Monday after being commonly deprived of the weekends with her for so long. It was what had become normal for Laney. However, she arrived with her usual sweet offerings - freshly made scones and clotted cream with strawberries - only to find the cottage completely empty. That was Laney's first-ever experience of being heartbroken. She drank lots of alcohol that day, well actually she obliterated herself with alcohol for many days that followed Margot's leaving.

She tried to forget Margo and eventually did, only when she realised that in fact she was completely and totally in love with her heterosexual best friend, Kate Andrews. She tried to fight these feelings as she knew it was pathetically impossible to imagine her life with her coke- cock-loving bestie. Why was Kate always attracted to a cocaine addict she would never know? She even tried to love a man. She stupidly moved halfway around the world with her undesired cock to fight her feelings for the woman she could never have. However, this denial only led her to becoming even more dependent on alcohol and pills, anything from Temazepam to Valium, she was popping them like they were going out of fashion. Laney thought it helped block the lesbian loves that she had lost. Can you believe she disclosed her innermost secrets to all her new, fucked-up alcoholic anonymous comrades? It actually made her feel empowered because compared to the sad tales she had listened to from the addicts that sat in front of her, her own tale really isn't that bad.

Upon recognising this she felt it was these sorry randoms that have forced her to think and that she has to get a grip with her dear Kate. She couldn't afford to lose another love and would certainly do her very best to keep her as close as possible. At least until Kate realises that it is Laney she needs.

# Twenty-Three

I arrived home to find Sadie was already at home with baby Kate. Apparently, the nursery had called as baby Kate was poorly, therefore Sadie collected her early. The house was very cosy. The fire was on in the lounge which instantly made me feel exceptionally tired again. I flopped onto the sofa with my girls and literally fell asleep. Sadie woke me a couple of hours later as she was worried the baby had a temperature.

Baby Kate was absolutely fine, it was her teeth. I knew this as her cheeks were flushed and she was gnawing away on her fists.

'Nothing a little Calpol won't fix darling,' I reassured Sadie. I was absolutely famished and suggested we go and get some fish and chips. As we ate, I spoke with Sadie about moving or maybe going to stay with Laney for a while. I was totally shocked at my daughter's response, as I was one 100% sure Sadie would be all over this idea. However, she was not happy about it at all. Sadie had lived here her whole life, in our humble little house, and was adamant that she was not going anywhere, temporary or permanent it was a big fat no!

I thought Sadie had become attached to our home in a way that it had become her family. Detachment issues? Maybe that was due to the fact she hadn't had her father. Or did I just blame Sadie's absent father for absolutely everything that appears to be a negative in our world?

Sadie also remarked that it was my own stupid thought for wanting to run away. 'Well dear mother if you hadn't been so quick to drop your knickers for your mate's old man, you wouldn't even be considering fucking moving.' Sadie's tone got louder.

'Oh Sadie please!' I responded with every effort, desperate to avoid another argument, which definitely went amiss. I really was not in the right frame of mind to be listening to one of Sadie's annihilations today. My daughter adored me, obviously, however, she had a wicked tongue and at points made me feel like the worst mother ever. I knew this was not the case, I'm a fucking amazing mother and when I am in my strong, normal mindset, I can ignore her mockery. But today I was a rejected, hormonal, pregnant mess and couldn't control my actions or my verbal unwanted honesty.

Sadie carried on her ranting. 'What was you thinking, Mum, for fuck's sake he's Frankie's fucking bloke?! Who does that shit? And now we all got to get uprooted and move! Well fuck you, Mum, you go. We aint!' The baby was now crying from Sadie's aggressive shouting.

I simply and calmingly said, 'Sadie darling please hush, you're upsetting baby Kate now.' Well that was probably like firing a missile at an opponent. Sadie went berserk.

'She is not your fucking baby to worry about! So don't try acting like you give two flying fucks! Cause if you had you would never have shit on your own fucking doorstep! For fuck's sake, Mum, why the fuck would you go and fuck the drug-dealing cunt anyway! It weren't some bloke at work was it? You're a liar! I know I can see it's written all over your face, so please don't fucking insult my intelligence dear mummy!'

I sat stunned, my dinner cold and untouched. My daughter was still ranting on about how I shit out and that. Why the fuck was she born into this family? Oh and then she ranted on about how if only her father hadn't selfishly died she may have had a chance at her pathetic existence. I actually wanted to punch her in her face. I lost it and Sadie knew about it.

'I'll give you dear fucking mother! I have done my very best by you young lady, sacrificed more than you can imagine. Whether I have made the right choices I don't fucking know but my girl I done them for you! And yes I have been sleeping with William since the night he found out Frank was sleeping with someone else. I am sorry I lied to you. But I needed to protect you from the mess I had caused. Unfortunately Sadie I love that man and I slipped. I am so sorry for that but I cannot change what has happened. And one day I hope you can understand and not hate me.'

Sadie sat quietly for a few seconds digesting what I had just said. She then replied, 'So why move?'

My honesty was flowing. 'Sadie please don't scream at me but I am going to be completely straight with you from now on. I never ever want you to think I am a liar. I am pregnant with William's baby and that's why I feel it best we move.' There it was, my naughty news out there for Sadie to digest. Sadie looked at me with pure disgust. She grabbed the baby and walked out of the house. Silence sometimes speaks much louder than words.

I obviously followed her. Sadie had no coat, no shoes and the baby was literally wrapped in a blanket. I grabbed a few bits, got my boots and coat on and drove after her. I found her at the shops sitting on the bench. Sadie was crying. She was in a complete state. I got her and the baby in the car. We said nothing. I took both the girls for a drive. I wanted to speak with Sadie and was hoping now I had exposed some of my own secrets, she would too. I just drove. I didn't really know where we were going. We ended up out by Laney's.

Subconsciously at this moment in time, I thought Laney was my brick, hence, ending up on her driveway right now. Why I didn't go to my own mother's was probably due to her constant derogatory comments about my life. The last thing I needed was any more negativity. I must look at the positives within my very own tangled messy life and stick a middle finger up at my mother's and society's perfect expectations.

It was very contradictory really, my mother was far from the perfect parent, she allowed abuse at every corner and then there's the very repressive abusive state we have to aspire to. Really, I asked myself, what chance do us lower little loners have when our makers and teachers are all martyr mother fuckers? Sometimes I think all we really need to hear is, 'I'm sorry I fucked up, let's change it, let's make it better, let's move on and up!' But for some reason I am slowly realising apologies don't come easy or even recognising any personal wrongdoing seems to be impossible. However, how the fuck can we learn and enter a happy smooth uncomplicated transition to a better being if we can't see our very own fuck ups? At least once we recognise the failings we can try to correct them, yeah?

I once read that destruction is essential. In order to understand the truth or the problem, as such, you must identify what is faulty, the point is to analyse what went wrong, the whys, the hows, the whos, etc. Then that way you can learn and reconstruct a new innovative approach to a higher being and fulfilling existence. Not the exact words used, yet you get my point. I think it was some French philosopher from the twentieth century who spoke along those lines, Jacques Derrida, I'm pretty sure that was his name, he imbedded himself within politics and education and I would say he was one of the most influential writers of his time and certainly, like Mary

Wollstonecraft, paved our way to a more equal living. This guy only makes me think of another Swiss-born French philosopher I once stumbled across whilst reading anything and everything to broaden my knowledge and answer never-ending questions on existence and purpose. Jean-Jacques Rousseau was his name, he too analysed society and its behaviour. He deemed men and women's purposes very differently to that of how modern men and women live today, he was still very much stuck in the Romanticism period where women really were just seen as second-class citizens, a silly little extra feature in their ever so self-centred man play! This is why Mary Wollstonecraft and her fight for sexual equality touches me very deeply. I will never forget a quote I learnt from Jean-Jacques Rousseau, now talk about self-righteous arrogant dictator, the sad part is that this reminded me of my poor mum and her own repressive existence, concerning really when you think about the timing and this only makes me question how far we have really moved forward.

'What is most wanted in a woman is gentleness. Formed to obey a creature so imperfect as man. A creature who was often vicious and always faulty. She should early learn to submit to injustice and suffer the wrongs inflicted upon her by her husband without complaint.'

You got to give him some credit - he could see the faults of man, maybe we could learn a lot from him! Love ownership! It has stuck with me and probably always will. This was hundreds of years ago when this thought pattern was around. I asked myself how many more hundreds of years are we, us weak feeble creatures that are called women, going to be perceived as a bunch of seconds? Pretty much sums up our fucked up society. Whether this was or still is the thought of our makers and teachers 400 years ago, 200 years ago or just a century ago it still very much reflects that of today. Ok we got the vote! Fantastic! However, I don't think that the tenacious woman of that time realised that man would only take advantage of our new-found equality and now it appears that the majority of women aka mothers of today don't have much choice but to take on two roles.

This fight for equality for women dates back centuries. Mary Wollstonecraft being one of those women, she was a strong advocate for women's rights in the late 18th century, she is a legend in her own right and is widely known for her controversial opinions and writings on women. *A Vindication of the Rights Women* is just one example of her fight for equality. I love this woman. Just for those who don't know her she is the mother of Mary Shelley the creator of *Frankenstein*. We all know *Frankenstein*! And then the very fearless Emily Pankhurst that once fought with her life for our freedom, we, their legacies cannot let these powerful, strong, fearless, dedicated women down! They deserve our vote even though, I feel we still have a long pot-holed journey ahead of us, our vote as a team will ensure our society makes the changes that these stars devoted and lost their lives for! Women's votes are not only important for future change but also out of duty and respect for the Mary Wollstonecrafts and the Emily Pankhursts!

Educate us feeble weak creatures and by golly we will be a force to be reckoned with. How many women do you see sitting on the political bench? Then this is where the coin flips; our superhero go-getter feminist legends probably never imagined that what they were creating was a society of lost roles, not just women but for men, certainly those from lower social backgrounds they were statistically screwed, they have lost their purpose, and in turn they lose their identity, they can barely afford to support their families due to the poxy low paid unskilled jobs that are on offer, hence the majority turn to crime just to ensure their children have full bellies and a roof over their heads, the state has failed here! Greedy capitalists have a lot to answer for! Wow I'm all for capitalism but not at the expense of exploitation! Is this another reason why there are so many broken and lone families today? I think there is a group of men that feel deployed, demoralised and certainly dehumanised, sadly they probably don't even realise the reasons behind their personally-felt failures! Many women I know feel exhausted, unappreciated and unloved. I know this as it's being discussed on social media, in coffee shops, at the school playground, the workplace etc! Do men feel this too? Who knows. But I'm sure this two-way loss of identity and purpose wasn't intended when our persistent polished predecessors fought for so much. Educate the weak feebles of society, and politics would have been a great start, at least that way us disadvantaged bunch of muppets would know what the fuck we were voting for, but the stiff, stuck-up genteel of our society know full well the day they put politics on the national curriculum is the beginning of an equal society! I was actually told by a tutor that I was articulate! Not bad for an underprivileged council estate bird!

I looked from the driver's seat back at my beautiful, scarred offspring. They melted my heart. Could I ever make both their lives better? Yes little old me? Scary really! Because living here in the 21st century as a woman and as a single mother it dawns on me that I am the only one who really cares about my child and grandchild's futures and their fight to be truly equally happy individuals. I don't want them to feel crushed! And exploited! And judged! Before they have even started! Sadie it seemed was already crushed! And so goddamn angry! Her anger came overnight, she was always the kind, sweet, placid girl! Maybe it really was just her age and the dysfunction we'd had to face of late.

I noticed that Laney's home was in complete darkness and now the security light had gone off it felt rather eerie. To be honest it didn't look like Laney was home as I couldn't see her car, but it could well be in her garage. However, now that I was here, I really just wanted to be at home.

I said softly to Sadie, 'Shall we just drive back home to ours?' Sadie gave a little nod. So that's exactly what I did. I drove with a heavy heart and prayed for peace.

# Twenty-Four

The next few weeks go by in a haze. Sadie seemed to have come round about my unplanned pregnancy and the fact I had been seeing William White. However, I had been ignoring Will - it was all just too complex. But still I felt rejected! Fucked up species us women!

In the back of my head I was thinking Will should try harder, like knock my door down and declare his undying love and protect or suffer the consequences together. Yes, I was clearly back on my princess phantom planet. As we all know too well that's never gonna happen! This is no Romeo and Juliet tale!

I have also disclosed my pregnancy to my dear neighbours. Yes Frankie knows and no she does not suspect a thing. They both indulged in my work colleague illicit fling. Fiona was more interested in the finer details, like name, age and fucking eye colour. I had to think on my toes. This bullshitting malarkey doesn't come easy to me. I hadn't even thought about what he looked like, my imaginary baby father that is. Stanislavski you are my hero, for if I were not aware of your acting technique, my terrible deceit would have most definitely been exposed and laid bare for all and sundry to critique! Considering Will's children live next door and he picks them up and drops them off weekly I had yet to bump into him. There really is no hiding my bump anymore. That's why I had to tell Frankie and Fiona. To be honest it's not been too bad of late as Frankie seems to be getting close with Tom Crane, Fiona's Tom. Interestingly enough Fiona seems ok with Frankie and Tom becoming an item. Apparently Frank is no longer acting the disco minge and is committing herself to just Tom. They seem so much more together. Maybe Frankie and Tom could work.

Still, I could not deal with the drama that would come with Frankie ever discovering the truth about William and the baby, let alone Sadie. Frankie would not take any of it lying down whether she had found peace with Tom or not. Frankie would still kill for her Willy. But for now Frank stays at Tom's quite a bit so at least she is not in my face banging on about William.

Sadie seemed so much better, a bit more focused, she has since made up with Jack which certainly improved her dark moods. I couldn't have thanked Jack enough. He has made my life a little less stressful, and he didn't even realise it, love him. Laney had been a great support and she seemed to have backed off, there had been no more intimate dancing delusions from Laney. Work was okish. I have cleaned more toilets in my lifetime than I'd ever anticipated! It's a job! Life was calm considering the events of the last year, which brings my thoughts to baby Kate's first birthday which is this coming Sunday. How can a year fly by so quickly? Sadie and Jack are taking baby Kate to the zoo. I would have loved to have gone however, Sadie, with no offence intended, asked if it could be just her, Jack and baby Kate. Of course I am not going to challenge her choice, although I did feel a pang of hurt and elimination. But whatever makes Sadie happy makes me happier. My mum wasn't best pleased either she actually put the phone down on me when I explained Sadie's wishes for her own daughter's 1st birthday.

My mum was a believer that Sadie should automatically consider my mother's wants. Much to my mother's dismay I have brought Sadie up to put herself and her happiness first, unlike my mother, she expects everyone to bail to her wants and wishes. To be honest I think most people, parents in particular, reach an age whereby they think it's their goddamn given right to put their own demands on so-called loved ones, whatever the consequence. Selfish really.

It was a boring Wednesday evening when the doorbell unexpectedly rang. No one normally rings the bell. I was pottering in the kitchen and Sadie was bathing baby Kate. I didn't recognise the silhouette either. I opened the door. William White was standing there. I couldn't control the tears that sprang to my eyes. William politely asked if he could come in. I stared at him in disbelief. He was so cool and composed. Dressed in his navy cashmere designer jumper and his Armani jeans, designer boots to match his celebrity attire, freshly shaven and smelling simply divine.

He casually walked past me, like he owned the place and sat at the dining table. I looked at myself and cringed. I had my skanky cleaning leggings on and still had my manky old green work tunic on. It was covered in bleach. My hair was bunged up on top and I wore not a scrap of make-up. I felt a complete state right now. I wanted so much to be angry with him but my embarrassment at my messy, unkempt and unloved self only made me a silent fraction of myself! William spoke first.

'Why are you ignoring me, Kate?'

I had no fucking choice but to respond. 'I can't deal with it all, Will, it's just so messy!'

'You are making it more complicated, Kate. For fuck's sake people break up, people fuck and move on. It will work out, Kate, if you really want it to?' William somehow managed to make this my problem. I wanted to scream at him but didn't dare. I wouldn't want him to think I'm more off key than he already does. I sat and looked at the only man I have ever loved and managed a,

'Of course I want it to work, Will, I just don't know where to start.'

'Well I've got a good place, answer my fucking calls! Don't ignore me, Kate. It screws me over when you shut down.' Will responded assertively.

I laughed as he was indeed right to a certain extent. How can we move forward when I don't engage? However at the same time he also riled me by the fact he seems to think it's me that shuts down, he is no innocent party for keeping his distance. Will is the one that puts business first. Even to the point of missing our baby's first scan. So really why the fuck does he wonder why I switch off? I did not ask him because I really didn't want to hear any bullshit excuse. I would only feel let down all over again.

So I simply said, 'I'm sorry, Will.' He pulled me close to him and grabbed at my baby bump and spoke to it.

'Well, we are growing aren't we? I'm your daddy, little one, and I can't wait to meet you.' With that William kissed my tummy slowly and then he grabbed my face with both hands and proceeded to snog me. He pulled back still holding my face in his hands and said, 'I will make this work, Kate, you are what I want, and our baby is what I want.'

I was overwhelmed by William's declaration of love but also very dubious. Where the fuck do we go from here? With that Sadie came bounding into the kitchen. Full of attitude, she looked at Will with pure hatred. Will spoke to Sadie, he asked how she had been and how she was doing at school. Sadie looked right through him and looked straight at me and sternly said,

'On your head be it dear mother!' And with that Sadie left the kitchen and stomped her way back upstairs.

I felt it best to ignore Sadie. William didn't take any notice, just gave a roll of his eyes. I was now getting panicky.

'What if Frankie or Fiona turns up? How will I explain your being here?' I say nervously to William.

'Stop it, Kate. Stop it. It's no one's fucking business, Kate. They will all find out soon enough anyway. And Kate, don't worry I will get you away from here. Just let me know when you are ready. As I said you should move in with me. But I know and respect the fact you have Sadie to consider. So for now I got a house over Wainscott way. You can live there. Close enough for Sadie's school and far enough for no unwanted dramas plus it's just through the tunnel so we can see each other at any given opportunity.' He said this with a wink and his cheeky William White smile. God I loved this man. How could I ever refuse his offer of shelter?

My next task is Sadie. She will move. Believe me I'm standing strong. I don't want my unborn baby to be denied a good father for the sake of others' happiness. It's not just myself I have to consider. I have been here before and I am not following that same deceitful path and I'm determined to live an open, honest, happy existence. The truth will most certainly be revealed at some point. Sooner rather than later.

# Twenty-Five

It was the middle of May the day of the move and god what a swelter of a day. I had a couple of months left to go before the baby was due and oh I felt it, the heat was immense for this time of year.

William had been his usual devoted distant self. God the man confused me. The thing is when I'm in his company he makes me feel so special and so fucking important, however as soon as I am out of his eyes he becomes almost like a stranger. Out of sight! Out of mind springs to my mind!

Sadie had finally agreed to the move. In fact she loved the house. Sadie and baby Kate had bagged the loft which also had an ensuite bathroom and a walk-in wardrobe. I knew that if Sadie thought there was an opportunity for her to get the better end of the bargain she would soon give in to the idea of moving. It's like sometimes you need to plant a seed of thought and let it grow, as such.

Sadie herself even admitted when Frankie has knowledge that I'm carrying William's baby there would be irreparable carnage. However, Sadie also reassured me that Frankie would have to get through her before she gets to me. I love my daughter so much. How fearless of her! I was actually excited for our new chapter. Little did I know what was to come.

It was early evening and I had just loaded the last load of big stuff. Well, the removal men had loaded the last of our home up and I just directed. Still, it was thirsty work and I was glad to be coming to the end. There were only the televisions and the mirrors to be taken over to the new house. I loaded my car with these items. Sadie was out in the back garden digging up the blue rose bushes we had planted about ten years ago for Sadie's supposedly dead father. She still wasn't aware that every year I watered them with blue dye, another little white lie! Sadie got a little emotional and decided we must take them.

I left her to it and shouted, 'Buzz me when you are ready and I will run back over for you.'

Sadie simply replied, 'Ok, Mum.'

I felt for my dear daughter at this point but blocked my guilt and let her do what she felt she needed to do. However I couldn't stand by and watch my daughter dig and sweat her own pain and sadness out from herself knowing it's all based on a lie. My lie.

The next I heard from Sadie was a couple of hours later when she phoned me telling me I should come right away. She sounded scarily calm but at the same time frantic with fear. I did wonder if Frankie had discovered something. But I did not want to jump to conclusions. As knowing my dramatic daughter it would be something silly like she had damaged the roots on the rose bushes. I know I sound unsympathetic but how can I sympathise with a pretend death?

It wasn't until I entered our empty home that I was able to gain any comprehension on the shocking situation that lay before me. Sadie was sitting on the bottom stair in complete darkness. Although it wasn't quite dark outside there was no light inside, which only added to the eerie scene. Sadie was holding her phone in one hand and in the other she held onto her shears, which I found impossible not to notice were completely saturated in blood and, to the point, so was Sadie. I did no more than scream. The shock of what my mind was digesting was torturous to the soul. Why was Sadie covered in blood? Whose blood? What the fuck had happened? My poor baby!

Sadie looked up with her big dark befallen brown eyes and whispered, 'Please Mum, don't be scared.'

I knelt before my firstborn and grabbed at her face with both hands and replied, 'What has happened, baby girl?'

Sadie looked at me straight in the eyes and responded flatly, 'I think I have killed my perpetrator.'

I must have looked confused as Sadie continued.

'Mum, stay calm but I have to tell you the truth now, I need you to help me.'

I looked at my daughter with reassuring eyes. She then proceeded to tell me that it was Will J who set her up and got her pregnant. At first she confused me, but eventually Sadie made herself clear. Will J ran a brothel and the night Sadie had conceived baby Kate was because Will J had promised a punter a virgin and unfortunately for Sadie she was easy prey for Will J. And now the wicked Will J was laying half cold dead in their  once warm lounge. Apparently he was released early for  good behaviour and on his way home he had seen Sadie in the garden through the windows and obviously couldn't resist sneaking up on her. Sadie explained she didn't intend to stab him with the shears but Will J had caught her off guard. He had been watching her and when Sadie had finished cutting the rose bush down she walked back into the house to find him at the kitchen window. Sadie said she panicked and tried calling me but walked into the lounge rather than past him to the front door and that's when Will J followed her and tried to kiss her.

I don't think he realised that Sadie was still holding onto the shears, otherwise maybe he would have thought twice about trying to seduce her. Sadie said she didn't think, she just reacted and stabbed him straight through the gut. The thought of being forced to sleep with another sick twisted hunter scared the life out of Sadie.

'I would happily die, Mum, than be made to have sex with some old pervert again. Still I didn't mean to kill him, Mum!' Sadie was losing her cool, I could see her tears and hear her innocent young voice quavering.

'To be honest, darling, I think the no-good piece of shit cunt is still breathing!' I responded sharply. I'm wild. I want to stamp all over the little bastard's fucking head! I try to keep calm for my tarnished firstborn. Fuck, Kate, think!

Think what to do for the best! I would leave the dirty little junkie wrong'un for dead but couldn't have that on my daughter's conscience. No way was I letting Sadie go to fucking jail. It was all too much. I could feel my body start to physically shake, from nerves or anger, I could not differentiate.

I had two options: get me and my dear Sadie the fuck out of here or call an ambulance and say this is what we have found. Maybe I needed to get Sadie out of there first. Yes get Sadie the fuck out. My head wanted to explode. I need to protect Sadie! I call Laney, I explain nothing but tell her to just come now and to my saviour my friend arrives in less than thirty minutes. Laney takes Sadie back to hers no questions asked. I assured her that I am fine. I made her call me when she was outside and I took Sadie out. I could not let Laney see the butchery that lay in the heart of my once-loved home. Laney saw the blood-stained Sadie but still she knew to say nothing and drive. I placed the claret-soaked shears in the passenger footwell. We couldn't have the weapon at the scene certainly with Sadie's fingerprints all over them, they weren't even ours, they were Fiona's. Another mystery that would need explaining! What a mess!

As soon as I was back in the house I telephoned the ambulance. With that, three police cars arrived plus an ambulance. I explained to the officers that I came back to pick up the rose bushes and found Will J like this. They asked if I would go to the station with them to make a formal statement. They did reassure me that I was not under arrest.

'On the other hand it would be extremely helpful if you could cooperate and answer a few questions at the station, Miss Andrews!' the shorter of the two police officers said this rather than asked. I had no choice but to act worried and abide by the boys in blue's informal request. It was hell. Frankie, William, Fiona and Tom were all here now boring their eyes into me looking for answers, like really my head seriously wanted to detonate. It took every last bit of my energy for me not to completely have a mental breakdown in front of them all and scream from the top of my lungs that I wished the screwed up little dirty mother's cunt dead! But I must say yet again fuck me and my acting skills certainly lived up to good old Stanislavski's expectations. He would have been so proud! My tears were for our daughter, William White, not your fucking warped half-bred, in-bred firstborn, that was my thought, but William only saw me as his devastated baby mother-to-be crying for him and his twisted pervert of a son. Little did he know! I actually wanted to stab William right now too. My anger was repellent. I never knew I had such venomous feelings. The boys in blue appeared to be my saviour that fateful night.

# Twenty-Six

It had been over a week since Sadie stabbed Will J. The dirty little pimp was still fighting for his life, the doctors said he was very lucky to be alive. Not that I give two fucks but for the sake of Sadie I pretend to the world that I care about the poor unfortunate little Will J White. It makes me sick to think my daughter and my precious unborn baby are actually blood-related to such a distasteful twisted young man.

Sadie had been extremely quiet. Although I have discovered the truth behind my granddaughter's father, nonetheless I am still clueless to the identity of such a sperm donor. I will make it my mission to find out who this old gruesome cock is and I swear I will kill him. William had been playing the devoted father and visited the hospital every fucking goddamn day. I still want to stab William, I know none of this is his fault yet I hate him right now. It's painful being around him. William had been popping in every evening, much to my dismay but he has the perfect excuse to be here, I have made endless reasons not to let him stay. And I thank God every day at the moment for not uncovering my Sadie. I know, pathetic considering what my daughter has had to endure but I do thank fuck that the police are way off scent when it came to Sadie stabbing Will J. The pretty boys in blue had explained they thought it might have been an old drug vendetta and that's why the young Will J White probably suffered the consequences of such violence. However, until they found a weapon and or if Will J wakes up they wouldn't really have any leads. Sadie stayed completely out of the way. My poor baby girl what will become of her? My heart literally aches for her. How she can manage to function I will never know. She copes by submersing herself in her studies. Thank God for theatre it really is Sadie's survival tool.

Sadly Sadie has ended things with her and Jack again. My poor girl can't seem to enjoy her relationship even though Jack is a great lad and so kind, Sadie just isn't able to let him in. To be honest can you really blame her?

My world has been crushed this last week. How must Sadie, my should-be virgin, guiltless daughter, comprehend it all? To hide my tears was becoming a common chore, the tears to be honest weren't that hard to hide, it was the fucking snot! So to say the least I had a constant cold of late.

Frankie has been over three times already. I know it really is due to Will J and my finding him. I think in a warped way Frankie feels closer to Will J through seeing me and going over the moment I found him. It was predictable now; what time Kate did you get back there? Where was he? Was anyone else there? So you definitely didn't see anyone?

Frankie, like the police, assumed it was a drug-related stabbing. I obviously did not discourage this perfect thought. As much as I actually wanted to put my coffee cup into Frankie's head every time she mentioned her little fucked up firstborn, I was controlled. What I have learnt about myself since this awful fuck-up is that I am no longer intimidated by Frankie fucking Twirp. This will sound crazy but in some fucked up warped way I relish in my debauchery against Frankie, it's like a weird revenge to what her son has done to my daughter. I have been contemplating whether or not to go to the hospital and put a pillow over Will J White's head, the thought brings me so much satisfaction. However I soon realise if I do that I will never discover the father of my granddaughter. Unfortunately I need Will J White alive, for now anyway.

The buzzing from my mobile brought me back to reality. I should have been at work but I just could not face it and at first I thought it may be my boss calling. That's one thing I have indulged in this past week, William's money, fucking rightly deserved as well I would say. Fuck struggling financially as well as struggling not to kill, what's the point when you don't have to? The fucked-up thing in this whole fucked-up situation is, in hindsight I would have gone to William to help me sort this but how can I ever do that considering it's his fucking son I want murdered? How have I gone from a poor, lonely, single parent, no drama life to an overcrowded blood,-stained, family-filled existence? I stroke my ever so large tummy and think what a tangled, twisted, tarnished mess he or she is being born into. Today is a day that I could easily run far far away with my precious offspring, far away from William White's Satan sadistic firstborn spawn.

My day got far worse. Will J was awake. It was Frankie calling me to let me know the good news. She probably hadn't even called William, she could still be a bitch, all said and done it was his son and to William's defence he knew fuck all of his son's gut-wrenching past time pleasers. He genuinely thought his Will J was a sad little junkie - if only, I thought. William was on a mission to save Will J and I, his baby mother, was on a very destructive path to destroy William's faulty blood-related mission. The irony is unbelievable.

# Twenty-Seven

It was now July. I had a week until my due date. Will J had been in and out of consciousness for some time. When he was awake he made no sense. I prayed he would never fully gain consciousness and if he did that he would be brain dead so he could never expose my Sadie.

I was enjoying some peace. My mum had taken the girls to a caravan site for a few nights, they were due back Saturday, tomorrow. Sadie was slowly coming out of herself. Sometimes, I actually see a genuine laugh. Still no Jack. But I think that is probably best for Sadie right now, she is far too vulnerable to be getting close with anyone, we could not afford for another to know the awkward depths of our world. Sadie has plenty of time to recover from her ordeal and meet a genuine loved one.

Laney has been absolutely amazing. I explained to Laney everything I knew, it does scare me that she is the only other person on this planet that knows mine and Sadie's darkest of secrets. I never told her about Sadie's true biological father. I think for now that one must stay buried.

Laney amongst all the 'EastEnders' drama has hinted that she has since met a new lady friend. Well, she said, 'new' but apparently Laney had had at some point in the past indulged in a very long affair with this now divorced woman. I want to actually snog this new lady friend of hers, excuse the lesbian pun, it really wasn't intended but I can't explain what a relief it is to no longer have your lifelong lesbian bestie obsess over you. It really was absurd.

It was early evening and I was ready for bed. I can't go to bed at quarter to eight in the evening I be up before the birds. I assumed William was at the hospital, as if he wasn't there he was on business. Every time I even mention or think of William and his ludicrous businesses I have to laugh to myself. Like really why do I fool myself? Like William White is some successful entrepreneur? Well I guess he was in the world of Class A. I hate him! And I don't know what to do.

It was one minute past midnight when I woke in the most excruciating pain. Shit! I knew exactly what this was. Of course I did. Gosh, how you forget the pain and then bang your brain rewinds instantly back to that first ever experience of birth. I am in labour. I telephone the labour suite and am advised to come in. I try William several times and to my frustration I fail to reach him. I can't call my mum, she has the girls and they are in Dymchurch, she would never get here in time. I call Laney. Laney arrives in what seems like minutes but it wasn't, it was at least half an hour. However, due to my pain increasing at a shocking rate I became oblivious to time.

We arrive at the hospital and within the hour I give birth to a beautiful baby boy. Oh he was delicate, he weighed just over five pounds and had masses of dark hair, my dear new born could actually pass as a foreign baby. God he looked like William.

I still have heard nothing from the father of my baby it is now seven in the morning and Laney has gone to get us some bacon sandwiches, I feel absolutely famished. I call my mum and let them all know the good news. Apparently they came back yesterday due to the weather being so bad. It had torrentially poured down for the last three days and they had all got cabin fever from being stuck in the caravan. So now they were all getting ready to come and meet our precious new arrival.

I tried William again, yet all I can reach is his voice mail. I obviously deliberately do not leave a message. How would I ever explain that one if someone else retrieved the voice mail? My phone was buzzing and the baby murmuring so I get baby put him to my breast and he soothes instantly. I check the missed call expecting it to be William, however it was my mother. I call her back to be greeted with a hysterical unrecognisable mother at the other end. My body drained from any breath. I feel myself hyperventilating.

My brain feels like a mixed wash on an 1800 spin. I cannot focus. Laney walks back in and grabs the baby as he is now screaming, the poor little mite had accidentally fallen off my breast. I stared at Laney unable to speak. There were no tears just frozen shock. It felt like an eternity had passed but it was only a few minutes. Laney had managed to soothe the baby with his dummy and a cuddle. I looked down and my phone was laying on the floor. I must have dropped it in the shock at what my mum had just told me. I pick it up and check if my mother is still there. The phone is dead. Laney is trying to understand what I had just been told.

'Is it Frankie, Kate, does she know?' Laney says in a concerned tone.

I flatly reply, 'No.'

'Then who babe, what's happened? I've never seen you look so scared?' Laney pushed me for answers. I stare, unable to respond. I could not allow the words from my mouth to form. I could not comprehend the magnitude of the situation. Here I was with my newborn baby White and dear friend Laney, and my first baby is currently being arrested for the stabbing of Will J White.

I manage somehow to gather myself together. The thought that Sadie is alone makes me sick. I feel torn between my new baby boy who couldn't possibly survive without me right now and my delicate broken baby girl alone and scared. Every sense in my body screams at me to go and save her. I look at Laney and explain that I need to get out of here and that she is taking me and the baby to my mother's right now. I have midwives grilling me that I must wait to be discharged. The baby and I are fine and more than able to cope at home. However the law is the law and I am stuck here until the registrar gives us the ok.

Therefore my mother makes it to the hospital before I can leave.

I still can't bring myself to discuss this morning's events. My mother managed to do that the moment she arrived. Laney was crying. Mum was crying. Both the babies were crying and yet I was stone cold, there were no tears left for me, only fear of what I was thinking of doing. The fact that little dirty piece of shit, Will J, was probably still laying in his hospital bed above me right now makes me want to participate in a murder act. Mum explained that they had arrested Sadie on an attempted manslaughter charge. They couldn't do anything until an appropriate adult was there with her. My mum said she will go. I hated the fact I could not be there for my baby girl right now. I had to be here for my baby boy. Laney then offered to be Sadie's appropriate adult. Without hesitation I jumped all over Laney's offer of support. This made sense, Laney was all too aware of the carnage surrounding Sadie. My mother on the other hand was totally clueless and penniless so yet another factor made me sure that my choice to send Laney was the right one. My mother couldn't afford a solicitor neither could I for that matter, however Laney will ensure Sadie has the best solicitor she can pay for. Certainly no duty walkover.

# Twenty-Eight

Although I would have felt better staying at my mother's this was an impossible idea certainly when I had two babies to consider. The house felt like a nursery, double of everything. We did pop into the police station when we left the hospital. I needed to just check on Sadie. They let me into her cell to comfort her for a short while. I told my daughter to be honest and tell them the truth. She did, after all, only act in self-defence, It was me who took over and made the decision to get Sadie away. 'Let the bastards arrest me!' I told her. The thing was Will J hadn't seen me so they were only interested in Sadie. For now.

Still, William had made no contact with me. I genuinely think I will put a knife in both William and his sicko of a son. You couldn't write this shit! I sometimes believed my life was that of the set of a soap opera. Frankie on the other hand had been hounding my phone. I have ignored her calls and messages. The woman sounds wild with fury. Fiona turned up when I was putting baby Kate down to sleep. She was laden with many gifts. Fiona was so thoughtful and had such a good heart, after all that had been exposed and yet she still cares. At first Fiona kept apologising for just turning up but insisted she is genuinely concerned for Sadie. Sadie had been a big part of Fiona's life and Fiona had a soft spot for my baby girl. Nosey was an understatement when it came to Fiona, she wanted to know the ins and outs of a ducks arse. I was totally honest with Fiona, I told her exactly what I had walked into the night Sadie stabbed Will J with her garden shears. Fiona wanted the low life scum bag dead too. Frankie had apparently been round Fiona's screaming her mouth off about her Will J and how Sadie was pissed off because he had, Will J that is, rejected Sadie's wanting him to fuck her. I can hear Frankie talking like my daughter is some little whore, Frankie wants to hope she gets a sentence because if I clap eyes on her I will scar the skanky cunt. She needs stoning for bringing that barbaric scumbag into this world.

Fiona makes it very clear that she will be putting Frankie Twirp straight on the truth of the matter. I don't doubt Fiona will have a fight on her hands, not that Fiona gives two flying fucks she really is a woman not to fuck over. All said and done she also has the backup of Tom, yes Tom is loved up with Frankie right now but for that type of man blood is thicker than water and he will do exactly what is expected of him. I then go on to ask Fiona to help me find the bastard that took Sadie's virginity.

'Please Fi, any little snippet of who he is. I want him dead, Fi! And if not dead banged up in prison for a very long time. I will never rest until he has been properly dealt with.' I cry for the first time since Sadie's arrest. I think it most certainly has something to do with Fiona's support. I felt so alone and useless right now.

'My dear Kate, I will make it my priority to get this noncey cunt and I will happily cut his cock off! I'll have pleasure feeding the contaminated piece of meat to my Polo and Bertie boy,' Fiona said this with a chilling grin. Polo and Bertie were Fiona's beloved dogs.

'Oh Fi, my poor baby girl. She has been through hell, how will she ever recover? Oh and not to mention that my baby granddaughter is a product of rape! The guilt, the guilt. Fi, I feel it crushing me! I should have been there! Where the fuck was I?' I am now uncontrollable, I have snot and tears smothering my face, I can barely get my words out.

'Has Sadie told you where and when it happened, Kate?' asked Fiona politely. As much as it pained me to say, I did, but this only made me want to kill the nonce even more.

'Whilst my baby was being brutally raped my dear Fi, I was cleaning some capitalist arsehole's fat house! It was after school on Sadie's way home early June over two years ago. I should have been there! My baby was just twelve, Fi!' The sobs drowned my body right now. I thought they were going to kill me stone dead. I continued to tell Fiona the sorry tale.

'Will J took her to a flat, god I knew the boy was a wrong'un but never in my wildest dreams did I think he would be capable of something so twisted! The sick cunt turned up outside Sadie's school and offered her a lift home but he just wanted to show her something first, that's what he told her, a puppy, he even said the puppy was at his girlfriend's flat. Well that was his tasteless way of luring Sadie in. Obviously there was no puppy Fi, my Sadie was as cold as ice when she explained everything to me and then cried like a baby when she told me puppy bullshit! You know how much she loves animals, particularly dogs, Bless her, so fucking innocent! And those wayward warped wankers took her innocence and now they must pay Fi.' My eyes were focused on Fiona throughout but my voice was desperate. Fiona hugged me tight and reassured me that they will suffer, she promised me and for me this was the most important promise anyone had given me in my whole entire life.

My mother was still clueless to the whole sorry affair. My mother wasn't the strongest woman around and seemed to run from anything difficult. I did not hold a grudge for this lack of maternal instinct instead I tried to understand her. However, that was never going to happen. My mother was a fragile, anxious woman, something I am not. I had learnt to accept her distant manner without feeling rejected a long time ago. Her detached silence only helped the situation, the less my mother knew the better, otherwise she would only end up in Shelley ward. This shit was enough to break the strongest let alone the weak. She was most definitely in shock. God only knows what she had conjured up in her head? My mother wasn't a silly lady, she could sometimes appear to be ignorant but personally, I think this cold trait of hers is her own coping mechanism.

Fiona ended up staying with me for the night, she'd had a few vodkas and thought it best to stay. To be honest I think she didn't want to leave me alone considering the mad crazy time that I had endured of late, I'm sure Fiona felt pity for me. I hated being a victim, however, at this moment in time I feel like a victim - pathetic really seeing as it wasn't me who was raped.

# Twenty-Nine

I didn't actually sleep a wink. I tried calling Laney throughout the night but only got her voicemail. Why they hadn't released Sadie yet, I do not know, surely she should get bail. She had never been in trouble, not once in her whole young fourteen years on this goddamn planet. The baby slept like a baby, I'm sure that won't last long. I was actually up more with baby Kate, she seemed so restless, poor little dot she must sense the tension. I felt like I had been taking speed all night, my adrenalin was through the roof. And god the night dragged! It was 04:53 when my phone started buzzing. It was Laney.

'Laney, where is she?' I didn't even utter a hello. Laney responded before I even finished my 'is she'.

'She is with me, we are on our way to you, we will be ten minutes. Get the kettle on, Kate, we are absolutely parched!'

Laney somehow in such dire straits always remained calm and collective. Maybe, I thought, this had something to do with her losing her parents so young and in such a traumatic way. Either way I am glad for Laney's cool approach right now. The next ten minutes felt like a lifetime. All sorts were running through my head. Have they arrested Will J? Do they know the pervert that took her innocence? Will they want baby Kate to have a DNA? God the questions were torturous. I see them pull up and before they even get out of the car I was straight out hugging Sadie, checking her over like she had been in a car accident. If only, I thought. At least that way her wounds would heal much quicker than her abused incarcerated scars. Sadie was the one who explained everything to me, all that she had been through and here she was standing before me as strong as an ox. The fact Sadie had exposed such dark disturbing secrets obviously allowed her to gain some sort of perspective on her situation. I must say, I was not expecting to see Sadie so in control and focused. It was amazing to see. All said and done I know my baby girl will be ok. The police have dropped the charges to a lesser charge, it makes me sick that she is even being charged, however, compared to a potential manslaughter charge it's a godsend.

Sadie was full of the police lady that interviewed her. 'Mum I never believed the peeps in blue would be so understanding, if it weren't for Detective Inspector Jane Duddin I would never have had any hope of this ever going back to normal, and Mum, Jane promised me she would get the man who took my virginity! It's the law that they have to follow up on what he did but unfortunately I will also have to stand trial for the stabbing of Will J. But again, she did say she can't see any judge putting me in prison! Especially when it comes to Will J White. Apparently no judge in this land could stand that scumbag.' Detective Inspector Jane Duddin had also explained to Laney that they had been trying to nail Will J for his brothels and pimping for a very long time, and this case will certainly help their investigation. Sadie said, 'This Jane lady gaver, did make it clear that this information was not to be discussed with anyone else, Mum.' Jane was a normal cop from a rough council estate in Dartford, she had a heart and she could see the wrong'uns a mile off. Thank God for people like her, because right now if it weren't for this Jane detective woman Sadie may not be so back to Sadie! It really is true that us humans need to be true to ourselves, whatever the shady scenario is the truth always prevails! And Sadie is appearing to be a true living example of this theory.

Sadie was now laying on the rug in the lounge playing on the floor with baby Kate, it was as if a big fat ten-tonne bus had sat upon my daughter for so long and now the heavy dark weight was lifting from my baby girl. I feel a slight sigh of relief slowly leave my body. I could not cope with my baby going to jail at the best of times, but certainly not for defending herself against such warped ways of life. Let's just hope justice isn't as corrupt as the streets we walk, that way we can all live in hope for a better, safer existence. Will J was still in hospital, apparently still too ill for prison. The seriousness of the charge for running brothels, a Section 33A, that's the official term, apparently ensures Will J is under police surveillance until he is well enough for prison. Until they find the noncey bastard that raped Sadie that sex traffic charge is in motion, as such. Not that I had a clue what all this meant but Laney's solicitor advised it was all good. Will J is looking at a very long time behind bars he even has armed police outside his hospital bed. The boys in blue wanted that little bastard as much as I did.

Frankie doesn't believe Sadie's accusations about her firstborn, however, she has stopped messaging me since her perverted offspring Will J's arrest. If Frankie keeps running her mouth off, calling Sadie a liar I will hurt her just like I intended to hurt her noncey son. The audacity of her over something so fucking fucked up! She, darling Frank, will be one sorry cunt!

Apparently they arrested him at midnight last night. The police are pushing to interview him whilst he lay in his bed at the hospital but some doctor is holding this up. Apparently Will J is still not well enough for interrogation! Makes me sick. Talk about ironic. My baby girl wasn't ready to be raped and a mother at the fresh age of thirteen. And some dozy dick doctor gets to protect scumbags like Will J White.

There was myself, Sadie, Laney, and Fiona all sitting at the six-seater dining table that I had recently acquired via William and his dodgy earnings. We were eating a big fat fry up. Baby Kate was sitting in her high chair and my dear son was sleeping in his bouncer chair. It was a lovely happy moment. Happiness is born in moments. Oh my dear little man who still hasn't a name yet. I look at him and genuinely wonder what will I call him. However, name or no name, it was the first time in a hell of a long time life felt breathable. I make a mental note to call my mother and let her know Sadie is home and I will say that there has been a misunderstanding, like I say best she stay clueless for now. I will tell her an edited not so far-fetched version of Sadie's misfortune.

I have still not heard a dickie bird from Mr William White himself. Shocking considering I have within the last two days, given birth to his baby son. Where do these men come from? Talk about detached. I haven't really had a chance to even consider my own situation I have been completely absorbed with my daughter. Maybe that's his poor excuse too. At least mine is a clean excuse unlike that of William's rotten excuse for literally dismissing the birth of his child and not even making a show, all in order to support a noncey premature pimp! Blood's thicker than water! Well this will certainly be the test for my children's father. I want Will J dead! And I want his father and my children's father to give his blessing! My mum always said I wanted the impossible. I always responded with, 'I live for the impossible, Mother! And nothing is impossible when we live in the 21st century!'

# Thirty

Frankie was aghast at the latest events, she was currently screaming down the phone at William.

'You silly cunt, like our boy would ever be capable of such whoreship! You got no faith, Will, not even in your own. Really what you need to be doing is shutting that lying little slag up. This is about your fucking own flesh and blood.' Frankie was wild with fury and William was getting it.

'Fuck off, Frank. What, you actually want me to get someone to maim the poor girl? You off your fucking head, woman! Look the old bill got evidence, they got an address that they're checking out now!' William was trying to make Frankie see what their boy could be capable of. Frankie was not impressed with William writing-off their son.

'What the fuck do you know Will, fucking a gaver now are we?'

'Don't worry how I know this shit Frank just listen, and no, no, I am not! Frank the boy is in it up to his neck, he needs help, mate! I have been doing some digging meself and he has been running a brothel but he's not only using the place for hookers he's also using it for perverts. Apparently he was earning three times the amount for virgins! I have even seen the little wanker's phone. He even managed to operate whilst he was banged up. They got bank statements, all sorts! It's all there in black and white, Frank. Again ask no fucking questions on how I know but do trust me our boy will be lucky if he gets to see 40 on the street!' William was firm with Frankie he just wanted her to know the truth, however bitter.

Frankie screamed at William, 'Why the fuck would you do this? He's yours, you should protect him no matter what you useless cunt!' With that Frankie hung the phone up. Frankie was fuming. How could William be so fucking sure? Frankie had to get to the hospital to see Will J. Frankie couldn't think straight, it was like she had been on autopilot for weeks. Why the fuck didn't Kate and Sadie say their bullshit version all those weeks ago when Will J first got stabbed? Because it's a load of bull. My boy is a lot of things, thought Frankie, but not a fucking arranged kiddie fiddler! She felt sick at the thought, she knew only too well what being a subject of sexual abuse really was, and her heart told her there was no way her precious firstborn was as wicked as his gruesome gramps. However, until the blue bastards have concrete evidence that Will J would ever be so corrupt she would fight until her death for his innocence.

Tom had been bugging her but she was too consumed with her wayward family shit to engage. Tom was great for her, Frankie knew this but all said and done he was a far cry from her only love, William White. But William had well and truly pissed Frank off with his believing such crap about their baby boy. Tom could prove a helping hand in proving Will J's innocence, he knew people. Frankie telephoned Tom on her way to the hospital and arranged to meet with him after the hospital. Frank also called in to see Tyler Turner on her way to the hospital. Tyler's flat was on White Road Estate where Frankie grew up, she knew she would find Tyler Turner's flat. She admits she preferred where she lives now and actually, Weeds Wood Estate for Frank is the better of the two. Even though her roots were White Road Estate born, she would never go back there. Probably two of the most naughtiest council estates in Medway! You wouldn't be shocked to see horses and horse carts floating around either one. Crazy little communities, although you were all pretty much in the same boat fighting for survival, you still had the hierarchies, the drug dealers, the street fighters, and the travellers they were the ones that owned an air of status and presence and everyone knew and felt these people!

The rest of the downtrodden bunch looked up at them like they were celebrities! How funny, thought Frank, she was actually fucking this little toss pot for a bit and yet she knew nothing of him accept he was Will J's closest pal. Frankie still asked herself why she felt the need to sleep with her son's friend. Her cheeks flushed at her memory of the shocking antics she had shared with the young man. Anyway it was no longer about her getting attention from every corner, this was about proving her boy's innocence.

Frankie only had to pull up at the corner of White Road Estate itself before she came across some hoodies and they knew exactly who Frankie was and they certainly didn't hesitate in giving up Tyler's drum. Frankie knew it was the fact she was William White's ex missus but she still felt she held her own whether she was with William or not he was her baby's father and that in itself earned enough respect for her to still get what she wanted.

So Frank was now driving to Tyler's. He had moved to the bottom of Ordnance Street in some council flat, a skanky, notorious place known to be heaving with alcoholics and heroin addicts. Tyler looked very shocked when Frankie walked in. Some junkie whore answered the door and at first she was trying to blag Frankie and deny that Tyler was about. Frank knew better than to listen to this wounded waster and barged past the sorry smelly state.

The place was like going back in time to your gran's house. Stripy pink wallpaper on the bottom with a floral design paper on the top cut in half via a matching floral border. A deep piled long-haired carpet, which one can only assume was once a cream shabby carpet and now a stained encrusted long-haired dark beige thing, my poor shoes was Frank's first thought. The place smelt of tobacco and was littered with empty beer cans and lots of overflowing ashtrays. Tyler didn't strike Frank as the type to live in such squalor as he was normally immaculately turned out. There was a strong pungent smell of cannabis, Frank suspected there was a grow going on in one of the bedrooms. Tyler was a sight for sore eyes. He was sitting at a small table and chairs in the tiny kitchen counting money, notes, and lots of them. Tyler adorned his usual look of fresh tracksuit, crisp white t-shirt, baseball cap and the latest trainers look, a pure Nike lover was Tyler.

'Easy, Frankie girl!' Tyler said with utter surprise. His face said it all. All wide eyed and mouth open.

'Well hello, Master Turner,' flirted Frankie.

Tyler responded promptly. 'And to what do I owe the pleasure?'

Frankie couldn't help but smile at the cocky little shit.

Then in walked the sorry state saying, 'Sorry T, she wouldn't fuck off.'

The meek girl that stood before Frankie was now glaring at her. Frank wanted to stripe the skank. However she wasn't in the mood for blood and tears over nothing. So Frank did no more than tell the poor girl to do one.

'Fuck off, whore, before I end up scarring that rotten face of yours!' Frank said this in her most sternest voice. The girl looked at Tyler for backup.

Tyler simply replied, 'Fuck off then!'

The girl did no more than walk from the flat.

Tyler looked at Frankie and said, 'So enlighten me then Frankie. To what do I owe the pleasure?'

Frankie stood in the doorway of this sorry place and couldn't get how such a young, little dick could carry such a persona? He was full of himself. Frankie actually thought he may think she had come round here for a coke-fuelled fuck. Oh how he was wrong.

'Look little man, don't get cocky with me. I am here on behalf of William, he wants facts and he wants blood so let me warn you Tyler, you screw me over, you screw William over and we all know what happens to dicks that screw Mr White over, don't we?' Frank was evil as she spoke and she meant business.

'Look Frankie fucking Twirp don't come round my gaff giving it the big bollox. You really believe William fucking White is the only fucking warped dealer out there, don't you? Well let me tell you something he really aint!' Tyler said this with a sadistic tone.

'You lairy little cunt, T boy!' Frank was in shock, she did not expect the jumped-up little fuck to be so cocky. Frank knew she'd best change her approach. William fucking White wasn't getting her anywhere. 'Listen Tyler you're right about William and to be honest with you the fuck-up don't even know I'm here, the piece of shit cunt believes all this bollox about Will J setting up the rape of Sadie Andrews. I beg you Tyler please help me right my boy's name, your mate, your pal Tyler. Please I need you.' Frankie pleaded with Tyler.

Tyler laughed at Frank.

This confused Frankie. 'What, what is so fucking funny?' Frankie asked Tyler.

Tyler laughed, looked straight at Frankie and replied, 'Look Frank, babe, the thing is Will J is bang to rights. He was running a flat over the estate and he got clever or should I say stupid. Well he had a couple of erm shall I say professionals, you know, the white coat sort and they erm offered Will J a price he couldn't refuse for virgins. Don't ask me how many Frank but believe me Sadie wasn't the first or the last. I'm done with the boy, mate. No good to me a fucking naughty nonce. All said and done I know I sell fucking all sorts but fuck selling fannies that aren't ready and wanting. You see my point Frank?'

Frank looked broken. The tears were uncontrollable. How had she nurtured such spawn? Frankie couldn't respond to Tyler. She sat herself on the chair opposite this young man that had burnt her ears with his tales. 'Please Tyler please what am I to do?' Frank wanted Tyler to grab her right now and take her to another fantasy, she craved his touch, or should she say she craved the touch of a man - any man right now would work. She needed to escape into an orgasmic oblivion.

Tyler stood up and was now in front of Frankie looking down at her, he grabbed at her face and said, 'Frank go save the other two don't let them turn out like Will J. That's the best you can do my girl.' Frankie couldn't help but kiss him. Tyler pulled back and hesitated initially and then he looked at Frank deep in her eyes and kissed her back. They were soon making out on the kitchen table. It was a hard, fast, forceful fuck. The only emotion felt was that of sadness for both their loss. A son and a friend.

# Thirty-One

William White felt sick to his stomach, he hadn't been able to eat since his discovery of his eldest son Will J's wrongdoing. William hadn't been able to face anyone. The night the police turned up at the hospital to arrest Will J for the rape of Sadie Andrews, William had gone into complete shock mode. William was on a mission to find out the truth. However, Mr White experienced for the first time that curiosity really did kill the cat. William got the truth from several sources, that was the problem, he didn't only get the truth of the matter but he got proof and at the same time shame, shame that he had never felt before in his whole entire life.

The thing is William had seen and heard a lot of warped shit, but none like that of his own flesh and blood, as much as William hated his own thoughts of wanting to strangle the last breath out of the little bastard, he also did want help for his twisted freak of a kid. Could they ever come back from this? William knew there would be half a chance if he hadn't gone and fallen for Kate Andrews and knocked her up with his kid. William felt another pang of sickness but this was guilt. Guilt for Kate and their newborn. Kate would never be able to forgive such a sin and William knew this, we were talking about the rape of her little girl, no mother surely would ever excuse such a thing. In fact, thought William, no parent could ever exonerate such a distasteful act, it was only maybe a little easier for William to even consider this as he wasn't the father of a girl who had been brutally tarnished.

Unfortunately for William, in this particular case it was his lover's daughter that had been prey for his own son. William knew he had to go and face Kate but at the same time Kate would be asking questions he just wasn't ready to answer. William knew it would be a matter of time before the identity of Sadie's baby's father was exposed but he really didn't want to become wrapped up in an underage sex trafficking case. That kind of shit sticks and he hoped for his son's sake that he would get a long time in jail as no one he knew would accept that rotten and risky behaviour on our streets and that his son, if somehow was let out, would be tortured to death.

William knew he would at least be able to try and salvage some sort of a relationship with his son if he were banged up rather than loose on the outside.

# Thirty-Two

I was exhausted. The baby had had me up every night for the last week or so. Thank God for Sadie this fine summer morning. My dear daughter had taken both the babies for a walk to give me some me-time. The bath proved a little grace and allowed me to indulge in myself. I hadn't seen or heard from William for nearly six weeks. I knew this not because I was counting but because the baby was to be registered by Friday this week.

The poor little mite was still nameless. It just felt wrong naming him without William's input. He was, after all, his as well. I was tempted to call William and confront him on his silence and challenge his distance. There would be no denying he knew the truth by now, maybe that was the reason behind Mr White's cold rejection? I couldn't help wonder whether William really would turn his back on me. Fuck it, I thought, that man's getting it.

Will J was safely banged up for now so I knew there would be no way William would be with the little cunt, the thought that he was in the same room as Will J whilst I was on the other end of the phone made every single hair on my body stand on end. Although the court case will drag, Sadie had already made a video of her statement so therefore she wouldn't be required to go to court and relive her ordeal over and over again. Baby Kate has had swabs taken and they have been filed for evidence against the pathetic pervert prick that took Sadie's virginity unlawfully. Apparently, Duddin and her team are close to catching him, however she cannot give me any leads, it would be more than her career is worth, she had told me gently.

Fiona has also been on the case. She managed to get her Tom to find out that Frankie now knows the truth and is apparently humble. The police had got enough evidence from Sadie, the address of the flat Will J used to trap her was found to be full of underage girls being used as sex slaves for the upper class perverts of our society. The flat was also that of the tenancy of Mr Will J White. It was like music to Kate's ears when DI Duddin told her the news. She knew then Will J White was going away for a long time. That, I could digest for now however, I still wanted his blood and think I always will. The news got better and better that day. Duddin and her boys in blue also arrested several professional men for having sex with minors in a brothel. Whatever, the dirty dogs will probably worm their way out of that one but more to the point the budding blues got DNA from all suspects. Therefore we are one step closer to exposing the corruptive bastard that robbed Sadie of her innocence and left her laden with unsolicited baggage.

I was as thrilled as punch. I hoped that wrong'un bastard was there that day, as much as that meant in a mad warped way that I was wishing rape on another innocent young girl, my desire to catch the pervert that screwed my daughter overrode anyone else's misfortunate path, as such.

The media was all over the latest muck of the Medway towns, the fact Sadie was a minor held her some dignity. They were restricted, the media that is, on identifying the victim of anymore shame. Sadie was surely owed that much?

I was now dressed and ready for that phone call with William White. The fact I really didn't know what I was going to say to him was kind of letting me forget the reasons behind this very long awaited contact. I did, however, know whatever verbal torment it was I would let it fall so naturally from my lips! William was getting the full brunt of it. I scrolled down to his number and like I always did, I stroked my finger along his name.

It was fear I was feeling right now. Fear of William's rejection not only for me but for both Sadie and our baby boy. I pressed the green button that allowed my call to William. I hadn't thought whether or not he would pick up, I had just assumed he would.

'Duh, Kate, you fucking fool,' I said aloud to myself. I did not expect and certainly didn't intend to be leaving such an explosive voicemail but anger got the better of me and my wayward tongue divulged where it shouldn't have. 'You dick. Yes, Will, you. I can't actually believe it all, I've got your baby! Have you even given him a thought? These were the first words that sprung to my lips and I couldn't resist a little snigger of a giggle. 'What fucking man ignores their fucking newborn for nearly six fucking goddamn weeks? William White does, Oh yeah fuck everything, Will, and drop us both out! He is your blood, you cunt! What hurts me the most is you have chosen to dismiss your new baby boy, and may I fucking add he is still nameless, yes how the fuck can I name him, Will, without you? Why the fuck do I feel guilty? You should feel the guilt Will, you and your fucking pervert pimping firstborn spawn! Aww, mate, I'm fucking fuming, wild fuming Will! What the fuck was you thinking? You've pretty much told me where your shit cunt loyalty lies and it certainly isn't with us is it, Will? I'm so mad, Will! I want to hurt you like you've hurt me! I tell you what I'll give you something to mull over. You see, Will, Sadie is your daughter, yes yours Will, your only fucking daughter and your fucking boy wronged her, mate, in more ways than one and the worse thing is you seem to fucking condone it! Yeah well condone that. Yeah Sadie is yours! Don't tell me you forgot our brief underage fling, albeit I was consenting I give you that much but fuck really! How did you never work it out?' With that, I pressed the red end button.

Now I was a mix of fury and fret. What had I done? Oh fuck, Kate, you and your fucking angry trap. He had made me so angry by ignoring me and the baby for so long and then letting me reach his voicemail sent me over the edge. God what if he comes over shooting his mouth off? What if Sadie hears? What the fuck have I done? My thought was now with Sadie. What would she do? Not just herself but Sadie if she ever found out? The questions were overwhelming me.

# Thirty-Three

William had just got off the phone to Frankie and he saw that he had a missed call and a voicemail from Kate. Frank was in a state over Will J and wouldn't leave him alone. All said and done she was the only person in the world right now that knew exactly how he was feeling and he couldn't not be there for her - not that he had any intentions of ever getting back with Frankie. She, however, is the mother of his children and he can empathise with her at least.

William decided to just call Kate back, he had ignored her for far too long and for that moment dismissed the voicemail. He was sat in the car park of his gym, a small unit up at the back of Rochester Airport, a nice little elite clientele for another nice little legitimate business of his. It was getting busy now and William thought it would be best to go and lock himself in his office and make the call away from any distractions.

It was well after lunch before William had got a moment of privacy. There was a leak in the bathrooms so he'd had to get that sorted before anything. The plumber was quick to arrive but he had a bit of a tricky one apparently, and finally three hours later the plonker plumber managed to fix the broken pipes. 'Funny it was probably only a ten-minute job and the wet melt made it a three hour. He weren't a silly plumber really, the cunt robbed me of three hours graft at seventy notes an hour,' Will told some of his pumped-up gym members how he reckoned the plumber had fitted him up. 'A costly fucking morning,' moaned William. That's when he thought, fuck, Kate rang me this morning. I was supposed to call her back. William headed straight towards his office shouting back to the guys that he was chatting to, 'Got a few important calls to make boys!'

William sat down in his ever so large black leather office chair at his ridiculously oversized mahogany desk and thought, this could be ok. No one he had encountered as of yet had even mentioned Will J and his appalling acts. He was sure people knew, stuff like that doesn't stay quiet. But at least for now he seemed to have a little peace on the whole sorry situation, he just had to somehow deal with Kate now. What would he say? Sorry was probably a start, he thought. With that William called Kate. Kate's phone had rang and then went onto answerphone. William didn't do talking into a speaker. Therefore he didn't leave a message.

William sat silent for a while and wondered whether Kate had ignored his call on purpose or whether she was busy. This led William for the first time to imagine Kate nursing his baby boy. The feelings this evoked in William actually brought tears to his eyes. How in all this could he have forgotten that his blood had been born? William felt bad at his behaviour and knew that Kate would be pissed with him for this as well. How had his life managed to take this mad crazy turn? William then remembered that Kate had left him a voicemail. He did no more than dial one, two, three to retrieve this. He was nervous although he didn't think Kate was the type to hurl obscenities into an answerphone, so really why the nerves? He knew it was probably a polite message, a can you call me Will or just her breath where she accidentally hadn't hung up quick enough. Either way William White was not ready for what Kate had to say.

Initially, William smiled at Kate's voice, he loved this woman and had missed her. Will couldn't believe his ears at what he was hearing next. Then he was interrupted with a knock on the door, it was one of his trainers, Dom. Dom was one huge lump he had to turn sideways to get through the door. He was a bald geezer with a load of tattoos, half-Indian and very good looking. William was looking at him with a blank face, the poor bloke was chatting away and although William could see his lips moving he couldn't hear him. Will must have looked like he had seen a ghost because poor Dom was flapping his hands in front of him shouting,

'You alright boss, boss come on mate!' However William just sat wide-eyed and in shock. He couldn't form any words even if he had tried. He jumped up and just grabbed his phone and walked from the gym. William just drove and drove. He ended up at his father's graveside. William sat in silence for some time. It must have been over an hour before William gathered his thoughts together and decided to listen to Kate's voice message again. He then looked at his father's grave and raised his phone out in order for his father to hear. Will then said aloud, 'Yes Dad, what a fucking mess. Yes your grandboy has fucked up big time! And can you believe you have a granddaughter, Dad and I have a daughter? Never thought us Whites could produce girls a! Well what do I do about this one, father? Fuck in hell me heads jarred, Dad!'

Will knew that it wasn't a good sign that he was effectively asking his dead dad for advice. But William did not want to start discussing this with anyone who was alive and living right now, it was all a little too overwhelming for himself to handle he couldn't focus, he didn't know where to turn and he needed to get a grip on the whole sorry situation. Did Sadie even know, thought William. He guessed not. But then he wasn't 100%. He needed to see Kate. William was back in his car and driving towards Kate's. As he pulled up outside he could see the house was empty, it was in complete darkness. Kate's car was absent too. William decided to wait for a bit. Surely they can't be much longer, thought William, they have two babies to get home and into bed. However, it was now gone ten and there was still no sign of Kate. William had called Kate several times, he had become impatient and wanted answers so he even left a few voice messages asking Kate to call him asap. The phone wasn't even ringing just going to answerphone, which seemed to frustrate William even more.

William drove back home to his empty apartment in a daze. Sleep was impossible. He had a very hot shower to at least try and relax him but that didn't seem to work either. He had now left well over ten messages for Kate. William was finding her ignorance a fucking serious pain in the neck. How can any woman drop something like that and then fucking switch off? William was going insane, he even rolled himself a spliff and smoked himself into oblivion. William didn't normally like the feeling of being stoned but this evening it really was the only antidote for William's wired mind. He was soon sleeping contentedly.

# Thirty-Four

It was a full house at Laney's. I hadn't realised that Margo had moved in with Laney until Sadie and myself turned up with the children last night. Margo answered the door in just a little silk see-through slip. She certainly was a striking, mature lady. Extremely small, tiny little elf-like features, her fake bosoms were obvious to the eye, a petite short-haired bright blonde waif-like creature. Her animated personality soon helped relax oneself.

I had never seen Laney so content and happy and there wasn't a drop of alcohol in sight, which I must say, it was great to see an alcohol-free Miss Meeks.

Laney and I sat up until the early hours chatting. Margo had an early meeting in the morning so therefore was in bed not long after we arrived. Sadie and baby Kate also went to bed at the same time leaving just myself, Laney and my nameless baby.

'Seriously Kate, you really need to give the poor kid a name!' Laney found it extremely hard to believe that I still hadn't managed to name him and this oozed from the tone of her voice, slightly animated.

'I know, Lane, but it just all feels too strange. I'm still coming to terms with my unplanned bundle of joy, so much has gone on Lane, I've barely registered my own life of late. Well he will have a name tomorrow won't you little man,' I responded and at the same time cuddled my little boy into me.

Laney looked at her with exasperation and said, 'So?'

I knew that Laney was waiting for me to reveal his name-to-be but I kind of zoned out. Eventually, I responded to my friend although it must have taken me at least a whole minute to. Poor Laney all wide-eyed and open-mouthed waiting desperately for my choice of name.

'Well obviously I have thought about it but I did ideally want Will's input, but obviously that's not going to happen!' I was gutted even though I tried my best to avoid the tears, they were already filling my eyes and grabbing at my breath.

'Do you really want the cock sucker's input, Kate? Seriously he is a fuck up mate!' Laney couldn't understand her friend's unrealistic wants and this was highlighted in her response.

I looked at Laney and said, 'Oh Lane, if you only knew the half of it, I fucked up big time!' I then really started to cry, the tears were soft and slow and although I was devastated at the way my world had turned out I was still very calm-looking, not hysterical but silently broken. Laney hadn't a clue about Will being Sadie's father.

Laney was comforting me and replied, 'Don't be silly, babe, none of it is your fault! He's a silly cunt who has managed to bring evil into your world. You need to forget about him and move on, I've told you, come stay with me. Anyway, name, missy?'

I smiled at my friend and replied, 'Marcus, after my great-grandfather!'

'Lovely, I love it, perfect,' Laney replied excitedly and with that snatched baby Marcus from me and hugged him whilst whispering, 'Hey little Marcus, oh you really are a handsome boy, aren't you.' Laney was now smothering him in kisses. This act of love and excitement for the baby had overwhelmed me and I then started to cry again, each breath that I inhaled felt like my last. It was as if I couldn't get a breath, panic hit me. I was sweating profusely and struggling to breathe. How could I go from being ok to a sobbing uncontrollable mess in minutes? I actually detested my weakness of late. Laney put the baby on the sofa and went over to me and stroked my hair and offered me some water.

'Please drink this darling, you need to calm yourself!' Laney whispered softly to me.

I was very breathless but managed to respond in a panicky low tone, 'I can't breathe, Lane.'

Laney knew I had got myself into a bit of a quandary and she grabbed at my face and sternly told me, 'You can breathe! You're talking! You daft mare, course you can breathe! Now just slow deep breaths, Kate, slowly does it.'

I inhale the deepest of breaths and slowly exhale.

'Yes that's it, in through your nose and out your mouth.' Laney's last words seemed to drag. I seemed to be calming.

Laney was so shocked she had never seen me so broken. But then in all fairness I had been through absolute hell the last couple of years, It had to come to a head eventually.

I felt so exhausted. My emotions were so irrational and my actions were so unpredictable. I hated being so out of control and genuinely didn't know how to pick myself back up.

Laney was making a hot herbal tea, camomile. 'This will soothe you babe and it's completely natural.' Laney handed me the mug of hot hope. I then looked up at my friend in a hopeful manner and asked Laney,

'Have you any smoke in the house, Lane? I could really do with a J right now.'

Laney looked at her with curiosity and replied, 'I do Kate Andrews, stay there and let me go get my green tin.' With that, off Laney went upstairs. God knows where she kept her stash, but she always had a stash. The hippy in her couldn't resist the occasional high, I thought.

I knew that a spliff would help calm my crazy state right now. Laney hadn't even asked why we had all turned up with half of our belongings. Funny, what with everything that had gone on of late it was more than enough for her not to question my impulsive behaviour. It was like she just expected it in a weird way. But really if I was honest with myself it wouldn't be normal to be normal as such after such shocking events. Even Sadie never questioned my erratic behaviour or my just casually dropping the fact that we were all going to Laney's for a while as a little break, she too said she was excited at the thought of just getting away.

I put my little man in his moses in the lounge which felt like he was half a mile away from me, we were only sitting in the kitchen. If only we all could live the Laney way! I plugged in his baby monitor just so I could definitely hear him. Laney had rolled two impeccable Js, one each.

'Perfect and thank you my friend,' I said endearingly. After a few puffs, I was stoned and it felt great, although my mouth was super dry but that was fine as Laney had now poured me a pint of vodka cranberry.

'Just what the doctor ordered!' Laney said with a stoned smile.

'Thank God I'm no longer breastfeeding! My first couple of highs in a long time! Here's to my baby boy, Marcus! And thank you my dear friend!' I raised my glass towards Laney in jest! We were both laid up on her sofas in the garden now. The kitchen wasn't really like a normal kitchen, the space was ridiculously too big. It was a dining area and sofa area and kitchen all in one, it really was beautiful to say the least. The triple French doors were all open so it really had that feeling of bringing the garden into the home. The cool summer breeze was gently lifting the haze of cannabis smoke out into the open air and up into the star-filled sky and at the same time it allowed us a little draft to keep us from being sticky since the muggy night was as intense as it should be in the garden of England and certainly so as it was the height of British summer.

Laney loved her music and right now we were listening to Whitney Houston's 'I Have Nothing'. My thoughts led to that of Mr William White. Although really relaxed, I was so tearful. William had tried calling but I ignored him and switched my phone off. 'What was I thinking? I've just made everything a whole lot worse!' I said this aloud, which was not my intention, well at least I didn't think it was.

Laney looked at me and responded with, 'How the fuck you could make anything worse is beyond me, my darling, stop fucking beating yourself up, Kate! Sadie's alright, the bastards are going down baby! Just fucking embrace your next chapter, Kate!'

I laughed and laughed. I didn't know if this was due to the alcohol and the cannabis or if this was simply due to Laney's unacquainted irony. Probably both, if I were honest, because this really wasn't a laughing matter. I stared at my friend and blurted it out.

'William is Sadie's father, Lane!' Silence fell between us. All you could hear in the background was Boyz II Men's 'End of the Road'. Seriously could the song be any more appropriate? Although not in the sense, but fuck it was insane. The song took me back fifteen years ago when I was pregnant with Sadie. How could music have so much power and trigger such memories? I guessed it was like smells, how they evoke so many senses and allow us to relive such heartfelt memories or maybe for some, those senses can provoke the harsh hidden histories of our souls.

The song finished and we were still sat in silence. Tina Turner was now playing 'What's Love Got to do With It?'. This only provoked my pathetic emotions and yet again induced tears, snot and gut-wrenching sobs. I needed to get a grip, procrastinating was not going to get me anywhere.

I was well aware I had fucked up! Any chance of a relationship with William was never going to happen. Well to be honest the odds have been against us since the off. But more to the point my baby girl, how will she ever cope with yet another traumatic truth?

Laney finally spoke. 'Fuck me girl! How? Why the secrecy? And who the fuck was dead Dave all these years? Jesus, Kate, you fucking floor me. Who else knows?'

I could only put my head in my hands and cringe at her every question. 'Oh Lane, really do you think I planned any of it?' Laney was sat in shock, mouth wide open pose. I then inhaled the deepest puff I could on my whacky backy smoke piece.

I carried on my confession. 'It just happened. I was so young and infatuated with him. I went to the over-eighteens' casino. They loved a young bit of skirt on the door, never even needed ID. Terrible really. That's when the Mr William White himself first noticed me. I went to a hotel with him, the Bridgewood. Jeez, I was young and super impressionable. I knew he had a missus and a kid. I was bang out of order, I know but I didn't care. Don't get me wrong I've well and truly paid my price for my innocent ignorance back then. But anyway, we were sleeping together for at least six months. In his defence, he thought I was eighteen. I never told him I was fifteen, for fuck's sake, silly girl a! I had an abortion before Sadie hence the date of dead Dave.' I smiled at myself and looked at Laney for some sort of support.

'But why Dave? And why lie?' Laney was still shocked and confused, her response was blunt and short.

'To be quite honest, Dave just rhymed well with the word dead. It felt appropriate. And how the fuck could I ever expose that? Fucking hell I genuinely thought Frankie Twirp would have cut the baby out of me. She was a hard bird and I was a little girl who had effectively fucked her over in the worst possible way ever. It was my worst nightmare when I realised that it was Frankie and William that I had moved next door to. My mum was living with us at the time, hence we got offered a three-bed house. I'll never forget the first time I saw William going into next door. We had lived there for over a week before we even saw any of them. They had been in Ibiza for a fortnight, I had later found out hence my not knowing they were to be neighbours. I was singing and dancing with Sadie in the lounge. I never forget the song it was Yvonne Fair, 'It Should Have Been Me'. I was even thinking of William whilst I was singing to the tune. And out of nowhere William, Frankie and Will J pulled up outside, unloaded their suitcases from the boot of the car and walked up the garden path right next door to me. I will remember that moment forever. I just froze. Sadie even got narky with me as one minute I was Yvonne Fair, singing at the top of my voice, playfully dancing with my little darling and then all of a sudden I saw them and I immobilised. I hadn't seen him since our last intimate encounter, Sadie's conception. I had avoided him like the plague. And here he was, my new neighbour. How could I ever expose such a long-held shocking child secret on my own doorstep, Lane? You must try to see, the tangle just kept tangling if you get me? I didn't mean for it to spiral so much and if I were honest I never really at the time, when I fell with Sadie, thought about the future and the consequences of such a lie! I just done what I felt was right at the time to protect us both. I could never have imagined in my wildest dreams it would all come to this!'

Laney simply replied, 'I see. But why did you never tell me?'

I saw my friend was hurt. 'Oh dear Laney, you had so much shit going on yourself. Fuck babe, it wasn't long after I fell pregnant with Sadie you lost your mum and dad and you was whisked away. And by the time I saw you I had already told my story. How could I change it? It was too on top, living so close to William.' My voice was low and sad.

Laney knew I was speaking the truth but still couldn't help feeling hurt that her closest friend could never have told her the truth about Sadie's father. But then again she had never disclosed Margo to anyone, she too had her own deepest kept secret so how could she ever condemn me?

'We all have secrets, I guess, Kate. But what are you going to do about it?' Laney bluntly asked.

I didn't know how but I had to deliver the news to Sadie and quick, considering she had already exposed the truth to her father. It was only a matter of time before William would confront her and Sadie needed to know before this happened.

'I've told William and you are the only people on this earth that know the truth. I need to tell Sadie, Lane.' I was calm as I spoke, which was good, and I knew this was because I was finally letting the truth breathe out of me. Laney somehow still managed to be shocked.

'You've told him! When? What on earth did he say?'

I remained calm and collected and replied, 'Yes, earlier today. And I don't know what he has to say. I left it on a voicemail message. It wasn't planned. I just lost it and got angry at him over Will J. It come out. Hence we are here, my friend.'

Laney didn't actually know what to say. She sat blank-faced and stared at me. Then all of a sudden, Laney was laughing and through her giggles she responded to me,

'Oh babe fancy leaving him that on his vm. Aww mate, you fucking kill me.' Laney whilst still laughing continued to say, 'Kate I wish I was a fly on the fucking wall when he listened to that bombshell. Fuck me, what a fucking drop babe, poor bloke his head is going to be mangled. Have you heard from him?' Laney was now composed and looking at me with a serious face.

'Yes. Ignoring him. I can't deal with him, it's about Sadie right now!' I replied sternly.

'Yes, yes of course, you're right. But Kate how the fuck will you tell her?' Laney was looking wide-eyed at me waiting for an answer.

'I don't know, Lane. How does anyone expose such shock?' My voice sounded broken. Baby Marcus was stirring, we could both hear him on the monitor. So therefore I went and fed my precious baby boy. Laney cleared away the kitchen and made her way to bed.

I took the sofa in the lounge it made sense now that the mosey basket was set up in there. It was 5am. But still we both knew sleep wouldn't come now. Laney was getting into bed as Margo was rising, she had an early meet in London and had to be gone by six. Laney squeezed her life-long lover tight and wished her good luck. Laney felt so blessed and still found it hard to believe that baby Geoffrey was one of her Alcoholics Anonymous groupies. He was now a seventeen-year-old recovering heroin addict and went by the name of Zacky, hence Laney was never going to guess who he really was. Little did Laney know that the day she confessed her lesbian affair to her AA socialites, baby Geoffrey was actually sitting there hearing the same tale his mother had told him a few years ago. See the thing was, baby Geoffrey was also gay but too ashamed to allow his conflicting desires to live openly in society, being an open homosexual was just too hard for him and he found a love in heroin. It was a big factor in his coping with his taboo sexuality. Margo, years earlier, had disclosed her own experiences with her own sexuality and told her son everything about her love affair with a young English rose called Laney May Meeks to try and empathise with him. So when Geoffrey had heard Laney's romantic tale he did no more than call his mother that day and tell her about Laney. The following week Margo went to her son's addicts meet and was reunited with her lost love Laney. It really was like something out of a novel. Laney's reunion with Margo had allowed Laney a sense of contentment. Laney hoped one day Kate could find some sort of peace, at some point in the future at least. She prayed that the lies were not too deep and hoped her friend could somehow salvage the mess. These were Laney's last thoughts before sleep took her conscious mind and left only darkness and dreams.

# Thirty-Five

William woke at the crack of dawn. It hit him again like a fresh punch in the face. He had a fucking daughter, a 14-year-old! And a fucking granddaughter! How the fuck could Kate keep something so big from him?

As William lay in his crisp white sheets he thought about Sadie and how she really was the fucking spit of his very own mother. Jeez, what will my mother have to say about all this? William's mind was in turmoil. Again he tried calling Kate but still he got her voicemail. The frustration was making him wild. William knew Kate wasn't at home. There was no way she would stay out so late with a newborn. Therefore she could only be at her mother's or her mate Laney's. Really where else would she go, thought Will? William needed to find out both addresses. Jack would know this information.

Jack didn't answer William's first call but he did on the second. William kept it sweet and simple.

'Alright boy. How you getting on? Tom said you doing great.' Will spoke to Jack about work first keeping it casual rather than questioning him straight away about Kate's whereabouts.

'Love it mate,' replied Jack.

William then went on to say, 'Good, good. Anyway, mate, I've been trying get hold of Kate and err well I was wondering if you knew where they were?'

The boy replied immediately, no hesitation. 'Oh yeah, I spoke with Sadie last night. They went over to her Aunt Laney's. Reception is shit out there Will, probably why you can't get hold of her, mate.'

William couldn't help being intrigued now. Just the mention of his new daughter's name sent him into wonder. 'Oh ok boy. So erm you and Sadie are all ok then?' It just come out, not that it fazed the boy.

Jack responded promptly, 'Yeah we are friends at the moment, Will. You see what with everything with Sadie she's not really into me being her boyfriend right now. But to be honest Will I am thankful for that. I love the girl and am willing to bide my time for her!' The boy was diplomatic to the fucked up situation. William admired him. He knew full well that he himself should at least understand poor Sadie's way. The actual thought of her trauma made William, for the first time, actually feel sick.

'Alright then boy if you need anything just give us a shout.' With that Will hung up. The bile was rising in William's throat. He leapt up from his bed and ran to the ensuite where he vomited down the toilet. Was his reaction like this because he had thought of such a dreadful act or was it because he now knew that this was what his flesh and blood had endured? Either way he had never thought about the intensity of the deluded act that his son had played a big hand in. Initially, his thoughts had been that of shame for himself and pity for his eldest boy. But now he felt violated that this happened under his own nose and even worse, to his daughter! His only daughter! And his granddaughter!

William showered and decided to drive to Sadie's school in the hope Kate dropped her off. However, it wasn't Kate who dropped Sadie, it was Laney. William watched Sadie exit the car. She certainly was a White thought William, how did he never see it before? Kate was right! How the fuck did he miss it? William followed Laney back to hers, he knew Kate was there, he needed to know! Not that he was going to face her right now. He had another more important business matter to handle first.

Once he had Laney's address William drove to see Tom Crane. He needed a favour and Tom could prove to be fruitful for this one. Tom was under some motor. Jack was standing over another motor with spanner in hand. They didn't even notice William walking in.

He shouted, 'Alright boys!'

Jack looked up immediately and replied, 'Easy, boss.' Then as quick as he popped up his head he went back down to work. Tom was a little slower with his response. Will could hear his voice saying something along the lines of,

'Is that you, Will?' However, Will couldn't see his face as of yet. Then within sixty seconds Tom was standing upright in front of him in his greased-up blue overalls.

Tom looked straight at Will and asked, 'So to what do we owe this unexpected visit?'

William replied in his most serious voice, 'Business, Tom. Your skills are required!'

Tom turned and replied, 'We'd best go into the office then, mate.' William said nothing but just followed. Once both men had sat down and the door was shut William got straight to the point.

'I know the name of the wrong'un responsible for Sadie and I want him cut up. Literally cut his cock off and stuff it up his arse. Torture mate. His hands cut off and the cunt's tongue cut out.'

Tom nodded at William and asked, 'Name?'

William slipped Tom a piece of paper with a name on it and responded flatly, 'Ya'll find he works up at the Alex. I'll leave the rest down to you. Call me when you got him. I will happily come and do the deed. Make sure you blindfold the cunt, Tom. Actually I think the nonce needs them cut out too, either way up to you if you want the bastard's eyes out right away, then feel free! If not I'll sort that one out when I get there!'

'I'll call you,' Tom replied.

William stood tall and walked from the garage shouting out, 'See you later.' Jack looked up from the bonnet of a car and nodded at William. Jack had heard everything the two men discussed, the walls were basically sheets of paper partitioning the space and not made for silencing.

Jack wanted so much to avenge Sadie's perpetrator and he was now thinking this could be possible.

Although Sadie was yet to discuss what happened with Jack he had heard bits through the grapevine and Sadie had only just started speaking to him, so the last thing he needed was to start questioning her. He did not want to lose her again. But he would do anything in the world to seriously damage Sadie's pervert baby-maker. Jack didn't ask Tom any questions just offered to be his driver.

Tom looked at Jack and replied, 'You heard then, boy? You aint even got a licence!'

Jack responded eagerly with, 'Don't mean I can't drive. Tom, listen, I need to be a part of this, for Sadie please.' Jack pleaded with Tom.

Tom stared long and hard at the boy. 'Alright then boy but I got few things to check out first.' Tom knew Jack needed this personal avenge! It was the poor lad's girlfriend that had been raped after all. 'I'll be back in an hour, mate.' Tom told Jack.

Tom was now on a mission he knew a few types at the hospital and knew that they would be able to get the bloke's shift pattern and then Tom could have him away in the van. It didn't take long to get what he needed thanks to Tom's human resources contact in the recruitment department. Tom had acquired the much needed information within the hour. The kiddie fiddler would be incarcerated and then dumped dead or alive, it didn't matter really as Doctor Wrong'un would not be in any position to communicate let alone ever wrong another again. Tom hated nonces and would happily torture them for a living. The gimp was getting it after his shift this Sunday coming. Tom let William know to meet him at his garage for about half eight Sunday night. The plan was to get the cunt when he finished work and was on his way to his car. The car park had a few security cameras but Tom knew a few guys on the security, the tape would be sure to go a miss.

Tom did contemplate whether to follow the nonce to his house and do the inhumane act there but too much evidence would be left. What with it being summer, it's still daylight until late evening so it wouldn't be a good plan to kidnap someone in broad daylight. Therefore, the dark underground car park was perfect for no wandering eyes and also the garage was the least suspicious place for a human mutation. Business would be closed for the day.

# Thirty-Six

Laney allowed me to sleep and didn't only take Sadie to school but she took both the babies with her too. It was well after eleven before I was back from my peaceful slumber and was welcomed by my wretched reality. Laney was hanging washing in the garden and the babies were napping in their bouncers in the shade. It really was an idyllic scene.

The rolling countryside surrounded them with its scatter of flowering weeds, bluebells, Red Valerian, and the beautiful knapweed all prettily distributed and perfectly displayed for our lucky eyes. The sky was the brightest of blues. It really was the scene associated with that of Kent and the Garden of England. Some days I felt blessed amongst all this tangled mess! The sun was stifling but there was a gentle breeze that allowed you to enjoy its heat.

Laney smiled at her friend and asked, 'What time do you have to register baby Marcus today babe?'

Whilst I pulled a chair out to sit down I replied, 'Not until three. I was going to ask if you could pick Sadie up from school later for me please?'

'Yes, yes of course I can,' responded Laney.

I looked at my friend endearingly and said, 'Thank you, Lane, I don't think I would have ever survived this shit if it were not for you.' And with a shriek of panic I went on to say, 'Oh gosh, Lane, I got to tell Sadie! How the hell do I do that?'

Laney replied, 'Aww mate if I could do more I would. But time will tell. Yes Sadie I think is going to lose the plot but in the end she comes away with more, a father, Kate! She may not see it straight away but she will, in time. Trust me.'

I felt some sort of relief at Laney's take on the situation and continued my conversation with my friend. 'I need another favour, Lane. Can you watch the babies this evening for me? I was thinking of taking Sadie for food and telling her then.'

'Yes, it will be my pleasure and I am 100% sure Margo will indulge in our tiny guests. Come on let's go get a coffee,' Laney replied positively.

We could see the babies from the doors and they were still sleeping blissfully. Laney was filling her coffee machine with fresh grounds. I switched my phone on and instantly it was ringing. It was William. I answered it, more out of instinct rather than a conscious action.

'Will?' was my only word.

'Kate, fucking hell finally. Look listen, I need to see you I'm outside,' William said eagerly.

'I'm not at home, Will,' I spoke back.

'I know, I meant I'm outside Laney's, Kate.' Will said flatly.

'Fuck, really? Really?' I replied shocked.

'Yes! Really Kate!' William responded.

'Ok. Two minutes.' I sounded surprised. I gave a knowingly wide-eyed look at Laney and made my way to the front door.

Laney mouthed, 'You'll be fine,' and blew me a kiss.

I was now sitting beside William in his new white beast of a truck. Otis Redding was playing, 'I've Been Loving You Too Long'. William couldn't resist but to touch my face and he automatically went in for a kiss. I couldn't help but respond. He tasted so right, I didn't even care that I hadn't brushed my teeth and was sitting next to him in just my bed shorts and vest. I pulled back first and spoke.

'Fuck. Fuck. Will, all that's gone on and we just carry on and kiss. It's not right. My fucking daughter!'

Will raised his eyebrows in shock and shouted, 'Yes my fucking daughter too Kate! But somehow you forgot to tell me for like fifteen fucking goddamn years!' The tears stung William's eyes and he looked at me for some sort of response.

My tears were flowing and I shamefully pleaded a, 'Sorry.'

'Sorry. That's it, sorry? Nice one! Does she even know, Kate?' William spoke whilst grabbing at my face.

'Fucking hell, of course she don't know. No one knows, fucking hell Will, really! How could I have ever told anyone? I was so young and to be honest fucking scared shitless was an understatement!' My response was full of remorse.

'I can't get me head round it all. It's one big jar, Kate. All of it.' William was quiet in his response and was now rubbing his head with his right hand as if he was in pain, not physical pain, but that of emotional despair.

I was so sorry and this was felt when I said, 'Will, please, I will never forgive myself for denying both you and Sadie of the father/daughter relationship you both rightly deserved and I beg you from the bottom of my heart for forgiveness and as much as I know I owe you a bigger, better declaration of my being sorry, but I really have to go and register our baby boy as much - as I know we need to talk! I need to get myself sorted and get back to Chatham for 2pm. Please come with us. In fact, you should come, he should have your name, Will. Please, for the baby if not for me.'

William was again now full of more emotion. This was down to the fact he hadn't even met his newborn. The last year had been rollercoaster after rollercoaster and now he had to do what was right and happily told me,
'I wouldn't miss it for the world! I will drive.'

# Thirty-Seven

William and I had a really nice afternoon together considering the circumstances. I managed to get everything off my chest. William was now aware that I was going to tell Sadie this evening. William did express that if it would be too hard for me I could leave things as they are. As nice as this was, I couldn't accept William's humble gesture. There were too many strong reasons behind me wanting to tell Sadie after so long. Firstly, after everything that Sadie had endured she deserved the truth and secondly, I knew in my heart that Sadie would never accept William in our lives not even for baby Marcus, but maybe she would if she knew he was also her father too.

I knew not only for Sadie to be happy, truly happy, that honesty was the only way we would all eventually find peace and then in turn hopefully one day true happiness will follow. Also the fact baby Marcus deserved a father was yet another niggle for me. I knew that it was now or never. To say the least, William was overjoyed with baby Marcus. There were at least a few heartfelt warm smiles and tears of joy rather than pain for a change.

'Sadie has a right to know her own flesh and blood and I can't deny her any longer not with everything that's gone on! And you have a right to try and establish a father/daughter relationship with her. I'm so sorry Will, I truly am and I promise I'll do everything in my power to make this right. I love you, Mr White!' I declared at our departing.

I wanted William to know that no matter what happened Sadie was going to know today! And from the intensity of our goodbye kiss, I knew that William had already forgiven me and only loved me more now that we shared not just a son but also a daughter. He really was a delicious and magnanimous man and all going well, I could feel the slight hint of a family-filled future with my beloved baby father.

We didn't get to discuss Frankie and what or when she should be told. As much as I cringed at the thought it was just as fair she knew the truth too, it would eventually get out and she was, after all, still the mother of William's offspring and the least she deserved was to hear it from the horse's mouth.

Sadie first then Frankie. I had thought long and hard about how I would tell my daughter. It would certainly be after the food as I wanted us to enjoy a meal together. I knew in my heart that I wouldn't be eating with Sadie for some time after I had disclosed such destruction. I had already asked Laney if it would be ok for Sadie and baby Kate to stay with her. Laney obviously obliged and was generous with her offer. Laney really had been and still was my saving grace. I could never repay her for such continued kindness and loyalty.

I hated myself so much for the pain that I was choosing to inflict upon my already broken daughter and prayed that Sadie would one day find it somewhere in her heart to forgive me for making such wrong decisions and understand that I was now trying to correct my own immature mistakes.

Jack was my next needed help. I wanted Jack to be waiting at Laney's for when we arrived back home. Jack was as loyal as I expected. I explained that I had to speak with Sadie and that Sadie would be in need of him after. He was a good lad, he didn't even ask any questions and promised me that he would not say a word to Sadie and that he would ride his moped over after work. I was as nervous as hell but felt I had the plan in hand. I was just finishing dressing when Sadie came in and asked,

'What's the special occasion anyway, Mum?'

I only heard 'special' and knew instantly my daughter had another shock to come. Nothing special about it, I thought, but disguised this contradictory thought and replied tenderly to my daughter. 'It's nothing special, my darling, I just want to spend a little time with you because I love you.'

'Oh, ok cool! Can you just put this on for me please?' Sadie's response was casual. It was just ironic that Sadie handed me her supposedly dead father's crucifix to fasten around her neck. The whole thing made bile rise in my throat to the point I had to run to the bathroom. The necklace was a gift from William when I had first started dating him, but I had told Sadie it was her dead father's. Sadie had never once wanted to wear the necklace, she had always said it was far too precious to lose and wanted it kept safe in her jewellery box.

'You alright, Mum?' Sadie was shouting as she followed me. 'Maybe we should stay at home, Mum, you look a bit off?' Sadie sounded genuinely concerned for me.

I was trying to compose myself whilst holding my hair away from any unwanted vomit that may have splashed up at me. I responded with, 'No, no, I'm fine, babe. I'm just starving and need food.'

'Really?' Sadie said, unconvinced and walked back to her room to finish getting ready.

'Yes, I've literally lived off coffee today,' I shouted out to my daughter.

Laney and Margo had taken the babies swimming for the evening at their fancy gym in Rochester, which was so kind of them. I still never knew how I would ever repay Laney for all her unconditional support.

I had text Jack letting him know that the front door key was under the flower pot by the front door, just in case Laney and Margo were not back to let him in. We were ready to leave. I looked at Sadie and admired her striking features. She wore a simple black dress, a vest-style. It was the first time I had seen her in a dress since primary school. The look suited her and only enhanced her growing curvaceous young figure. The crucifix hung around her neck and sat perfectly within the neckline of the dress. She couldn't quite give up the tomboy in her completely, though, I thought, because Sadie had somehow managed to adorn her converse high tops with the outfit. To say the least, Sadie looked cute and cool.

As we left the house she also grabbed her black zip hoodie that hung so casually over the banister at the bottom of Laney's whirling grand stair case and yes you could call the enormous architecture a case as that's exactly what it was. The dress was now lost behind an oversized piece of black cloth. How she wore that in this heat was beyond me. However, Sadie's amazing thick, dark, long hair allowed the girly girl to shine above all the black that she wore. As for her insanely long black lashes they only enhanced her oversized almond-shaped brown eyes. Her natural tan simply complimented Sadie's beauty. And now I felt I was about to break this strikingly beautiful mother/daughter bond that I had fought so hard for. I so much wanted for my relationship with Sadie to be so much more than that of mine and my own mother.

I had not seen her for at least three weeks, she was so wrapped up in the church she couldn't give a flying fuck how anyone else was doing. I told her that Will J had tried it on with Sadie and that she had lashed out at him. My mother was always gullible. But more to the point I had just had a new baby and my mother has only seen him three times. He will be seven weeks tomorrow. God knows how she will take the news of William being the father of both my children.

# Thirty-Eight

We were at Frankie and Benny's in Maidstone. Throughout our meal I sat across from Sadie wondering how the hell to even broach the subject. My darling daughter seemed so carefree and happy. All she spoke about was starting college next September, the excitement oozed off Sadie. She was planning to study drama and theatre, dance, English literature and Spanish. As long as she got an A to C in her GCSEs Sadie would be accepted into college.

I didn't doubt my beautiful daughter, I knew in my heart that her destiny was to be a star. Although I did hope that my news wouldn't crush this dream. I do think to myself, if Sadie can rise from rape she will rise from anything. Whilst we ate pudding I brought the conversation up about my being so young when I was pregnant with her. Sadie knew that I was sixteen when I had had her which meant I was a little older than her now. My intention was to highlight to Sadie how stupid and naïve I was compared to her at a similar age, however, I don't think she got that as she responded with,

'It was your choice though, Mum, to have sex and a baby. It wasn't mine!'

I wanted to scream. I was so angry those dirty bastards had robbed my daughter of so much although ninety percent of the time Sadie appeared to be coping so well but when she said things like this it would only prove that she was far from over her ordeal. I want those pieces of noncey cunts dead and I won't settle until it's done.

I reached out to touch my daughter's hand and sensitively replied, 'I know baby girl, I know.' The waiter interrupted the conversation, thank God, I thought.

'Anything else ladies?' He spoke with a foreign accent, I couldn't place it.

'No, no, thank you. Could we have the bill though please?' I quickly responded.

The waiter politely replied, 'Of course, madam,' and then walked away leaving silence at our table.

We were back in the car when Sadie asked me again how I met her father. Well if this wasn't my fucking cue then I didn't know what was. I took the biggest breath and said,

'Well if I am honest with you, Sadie, I've been wanting to talk to you about that for a very long time. What is it you remember about the story, Sadie?'

Sadie still didn't look fazed by my response. She carried on playing with the cd player and said, 'Erm, you met at a club and then the next you heard he had had a crash and died. Yeah, I guess that's it in a nutshell.'

'Sadie, I want you to listen carefully to me and please let me finish. Please,' I pleaded with her daughter.

'To be honest, Mum, you're freaking me out just speaking like that.' Sadie spoke with confusion and a slight giggle whilst looking at me with a puzzled expression.

'Please, Sadie, I need you not to freak. I need you to listen and I need to stress to you how sorry I am and nothing I will say will ever be able to show you how sorry I am. I fucked up Sadie and you were caught up in the middle.' I spoke clearly.

'Mum, leave it out you're the best thing that could ever have happened to me. You could never hurt me, Mum. Fucking hell, don't you think that.' Sadie couldn't quite take my efforts at a confession seriously, which only made me feel more guilt. But I was determined Sadie would listen to me and I could get this over with once and for all.

'Sadie, please just listen. This is so hard for me so please.' I pleaded again.

'Ok, Mum, just say it then,' Sadie replied.

'Aww, my dear Sadie, please promise me you will one day forgive me?' I asked her.

Sadie looked at me and reassuringly replied, 'Mum my life wouldn't exist if it were not for you. I will always love you and no matter what has happened I could always forgive you, so just spit it out, surely it can't be that bad.'

I glanced at my daughter and the tears already blurred my vision. 'Oh baby it's bad and I do hope you can somehow find it in you to forgive my fuck up. Baby, the thing is you were right I did meet your father in a club but the thing, the thing is, Sadie, he never had a car crash and he never died. I'm just so sorry. I'm so sorry.'

Sadie sat quiet for what felt like twenty minutes but it really was only about sixty seconds and then she looked straight at me and said,

'So ya basically telling me my father is not dead but he is alive?'

Still looking ahead, I replied a flat, 'Yes.'

Sadie started to laugh, which really confused the hell out of me. Sadie was laughing hysterically however, she still managed to speak.

'What the fuck, Mum? I can't believe this shit! Why would you?' Sadie was now composed and sat in disbelief.

I filled the silence. 'There are lots of reasons I've never been able to tell you the truth, Sadie, about your father. And I do hope that one day you will understand my keeping this from you.' Before I could finish what I had to say Sadie interrupted.

'So my dad's alive? Where is he? Who is he? And more to the point, do I know him, Mum?' Sadie was looking to me for answers, answers I didn't know if I was ready to expose yet. I knew I had no choice but to finish what I had started.

'Oh, Sadie.' I could not control my tears as much as I tried, they were oozing from my very tired eyes. I knew this wasn't going to end pretty. I struggled to say any more.

'Mum, just spit it out, seriously you tell me I have a dad, a fucking living, breathing, walking dad and that's it.' Sadie sounded baffled.

'No darling, that's not just it. I'm trying, it's just so goddamn fucking hard, Sadie. I don't want to lose you! But if I am honest I know that will happen.' I pulled the car onto Laney's drive, looked at my daughter and grabbed her face in my hands, and in a heartfelt desperate manner I told Sadie the identity and tale of her father. 'Listen, what you need to know is I love you with all my heart and all my decisions whether they were right or wrong I done for the best at the time. Now listen to me carefully after I tell you who he is I think you will need time and I get that, Sadie, so Laney has said you can stay here with her and I will go home.' I was nearly there but Sadie pushed my hands away and said,

'For fuck's sake, Mother, ya freaking me out, why would I not want to be around you or should I be asking what it is you have done so bad to lie for so long and why would you say my father was dead? This is all too fucked!' Sadie was about to get out of the car, however,
I grabbed her arm and pleaded with her.

'Oh my precious girl I want you to come home with me, of course I do but I don't know if you will! Sadie I have fucked up! Yes you are 100% right it's fucked and it's my own doing. But I'm trying my best now to be honest and to try and salvage the rest. I had a fling, Sadie, with a man who was quite a bit older than me but the thing was he was with someone, Sadie, he already had a kid. I didn't want to be the cause of another broken family. Well that's not the whole reason that was just part of it. If I'm honest it was circumstances, and if we hadn't lived so close to your biological father maybe I would have told you sooner, and him for that fact! Sadie, I'm sorry, your father is William, you and baby Marcus have the same dad!' My voice broke at my last words and the tears were soon flowing again.

Sadie was silent. She said nothing but walked from the car without giving me a second glance.

# Thirty-Nine

Frankie had been trying to get hold of Tom. It was late Sunday evening and she hadn't been able to reach him for nearly two days. She popped round to his mother's house earlier to see if she had seen or heard anything from him. Of course Tom had spoken with his mother. Fiona couldn't wait to let Frankie know she is still his number one, you could hear it in her voice, that sarcastic tone that she often adopts.

'Yeah he phoned me yesterday morning, love, said he wasn't feeling too well and not to worry if I don't hear from him for a couple days! Don't be needy, Frankie, it's not an attractive trait! He's got a bit of man flu and is probably still in bed. I'm sure he'll call you when he needs a cuddle, Frankie!'

This only riled Frankie even more. Fiona was so patronising. How can he let his mother know that he is ok but not his lover? Frankie was feeling extra lonely, what with everything that had taken place the last couple of months. She no longer had Kate to pour her heart out to. Frankie had lost a good friend all because of her warped son. Frankie wanted so much to rewind the past. She decided that she would send Kate a message asking for her forgiveness and her friendship. Kate had probably been the only consistently honest person in her life and the thought of losing her as a friend made Frankie emotional. She hadn't even met her new baby boy and this upset Frankie too, she had become very fond of Sadie and felt she had lost out in getting to know Kate's new baby. If only she had been able to divorce her own mother at least that way Will J would never have been exposed to the seedy world of brothels and prostitution and maybe he would never have felt it was acceptable to be a part of such a deluded bunch.

Since Will J's arrest Frankie hadn't spoken to her mother or let John Boy and baby Josh around her. Although her mother hadn't been arrested for any part in the Sadie saga, Frankie knew her mother had introduced Will J to the world of brothels and would never be able to forgive her mother for this. Hence the reason behind her not allowing her youngest two boys around her anymore. The last thing Frankie wanted was her baby boys going down the same path as their older brother. Frankie put baby Josh to bed and told John Boy to watch him. For once she was not going out on the lash, she was going to check on Tom. Frankie stopped at the Co-op on her way and purchased some Lemsip and Covonia, what with him feeling poorly maybe over the counter drugs would help make him feel a little bit better, thought Frankie. At times Frankie just craved to be loved by someone and right now she thought Tom could temporarily satisfy this need. She knows in her heart that it's a means to an end, just until William forgives her, if

William ever forgives her. Still, there was a slight chance out of all this shit that something good can come, thought Frankie. As William and Frankie are the only two people who could understand their own shame at their own son's warped and disgusting behaviour, this alone, she hoped, could be something that pulled William back to her again. For now though she was safe with Tom. She knew he would pretty much do anything for her. Frankie proceeded to drive to Tom's house. However, when she passed his garage she noticed that both his van and car were parked on the forecourt and to her surprise and annoyance so was William's car. Frankie did no more than do a U-turn and pulled up outside the garage. As soon as Frank got out of the car she could hear raised voices.

'Tom it's me, Frank. Will, is that you too? Will, what the fuck are you doing here?' Frankie knew she heard William's voice and couldn't help but wonder why the two men would be locked up in the garage together! Silence. Pure silence no more muffled sounds. However, Frankie was getting louder. 'Don't treat me like some sort a cunt, I can hear yas! Just open the fucking door or I will cause such a drama you'll have the gavers here within seconds!' Frank meant every word.

Tom and William knew that she was more than capable of creating a scene and had no choice but to let her in. Frankie could never have been prepared for what she was about to see. Tom stood in front of her and explained this was not supposed to be for her eyes and she shouldn't be turning up here unannounced. Frankie screamed at the sight of the butchered body that sat before her. The scene was like something from a Freddy Krueger movie. There was a naked man tied to a chair, the man had been tortured, he had not a single hair left on his head which was red raw, his skull visible to the naked eye, it would appear that he had been scalped. The poor bloke's eyes were also missing; all that was left were deep dark bloody holes with red tear-stained cheeks, his hands were severed off, they were now just red bloodied jagged stumps that hung loosely in front of the half-mauled man and it would appear that William was just about to cut his manhood off. The bloke was gagged so it was just an insane animalistic noise that came from him. But then Frankie noticed the poor creature's tongue lay beneath her feet, she could not control the vomit that was now erupting from her body.

Frankie had been witness to some violent times in her life but this topped anything that she had ever encountered since arriving in this god forsaken world. The place was a complete blood bath. William looked as if he was enjoying his sadistic act. His eyes were glazed over, she didn't think he even realised she was there let alone cared about what she had to witness. Frankie couldn't believe what her eyes were showing her. William was now untying the feet of the dismembered body, which in turn meant the poor bloke fell flat on his face, and with that, William shoved something up the man's arse. Fuck, it was the geezer's own cock. Frankie wasn't sure what she was hearing next yet the shock of what she had stumbled upon still wasn't enough to prepare her for what she was about to discover.

'You noncey cunt, thought you would get away with screwing my daughter, did ya?' William's words were like a knife cutting through Frankie's stomach. Frankie felt like her head was going to explode. Daughter! Daughter! Daughter, was all that she heard. She completely forgot about the carnage that was surrounding her. Although most people would be freaking at such horrific violence, Frankie's mind was only focused on one thing. Next thing Jack appeared out of nowhere with a hose and started to attempt to wash the gruesome blood bath away. Tom was dragging what was left of the bloke into his van. The blood splattered shutters were now wide open for all the world to see, which Frankie thought only gave the scene that was unfolding before her a likeness to that of a theatre stage, the dark night light from the outside world bursting in making it more like a sadistic theatrical illusion than her own reality.

William was at the back of the garage stripping his clothes off. Jack was hosing William down. Frankie noticed William's black overnight Gucci bag sitting on the roof of another car in the garage. They were all clearly prepared and knew their individual duties and seemed to adhere to them perfectly. Tom was now telling Jack to go with William and that he would see him tomorrow same time as normal. Tom said this like it was the end of another casual greasy day under the bonnet rather than a bloody massacre in a slaughter house. Tom then looked at Frankie who was just stood silently staring blankly at them all.

'Come on girl, you need to go too. I'll call ya in a couple hours. I got a few things to sort out first.' Tom was so cold and blunt. William didn't say a word just ensured he was immaculate. As William and Jack went to leave the garage, William looked back at Frank and shouted at her,

'Come on. Now!' As soon as William spoke to Frankie she saw red and couldn't restrain her mouth any longer.

'Like I'm some sort of fucking lap dog a! No, I don't fucking think so! Dogs, surely they get treated with more fucking respect! Fucking dogs, you're the only fucking dog in here, William Fucking White!' Frankie seemed to be talking in riddles. William was becoming inpatient.

'Stop running your mouth Frank and fucking move. We need to get the fuck out of here!' Tom was now in the van with the half-dead butchered body, all ready to go and disperse of the sorry mess. They really didn't need Frankie causing attention now.

'Running my mouth! Fucking daughter! Daughter, Will! What the fuck? You think I am some sort of cunt! Daughter! Daughter! Daughter!' Frankie had lost control and was now running at William and punching him. William stood in shock. It took Tom, who jumped out of the van at such a speed, and Jack to remove Frankie from William and get her in the van with Tom. This was not the plan and Tom was not best pleased with the ordeal but he had no other choice than to take Frankie with him. He needed to get this over and done with and then get the van back to the garage before one of William's runners comes over and torches the place. All evidence burnt, burnt to a crisp. Along with his beloved business. Gone.

Tom wanted to strike Frankie. She had managed to rile Tom and lure him out of control. Time was precious right now and this silly wayward cunt was causing him more drama than she was worth. Keeping on fucking mumbling shit over her ex wasn't exactly helping Tom's anger towards her either. At any moment he thought he might just strangle the whining whore of a woman that he had somehow managed to get himself tangled up in. Fucking coke had a lot to answer for, thought Tom. He couldn't take Frankie's screams any longer so he gave her a quick backhander, which instantly knocked her out.

'Peace at fucking last!' he said out loud to himself and continued to drive in the dark of the night not knowing what disaster his next destination would bring him.

# Forty

It was Sunday night and I was at home with baby Marcus and William. Sadie had ignored all my calls since I had told her about her father. I knew Sadie was ok. I had spoken with Laney daily who reassured me that Sadie was fine. Jack had been by her side and seemed to be distracting Sadie from any dark moods. But still Sadie hadn't mentioned anything to Laney about why she and I were not talking.

To be honest, I knew that Sadie knew Laney was all too aware of the truth and Sadie would at some point go to Laney for advice. William had turned up unexpectedly late. I hadn't realised how much I had missed him. To feel his touch was like that of breathing in air for the very first time after being suffocated for a decade. I would still experience those tight knots in my stomach whenever I was so close to William, I yearned for his touch. His eyes bored deep into my soul and I craved him like that of a heroin addict needing opium.

The throbbing that I felt beneath my delicate box was insatiable. We hadn't had sex since before baby Marcus was here. I needed his hardness to release my desires and fulfil my deep, dark, depressed frustrations. William seemed to know and understand my wants. We didn't even speak, we were too wrapped up in each other physically to feel the need to communicate verbally. William was more forceful than usual which meant my senses were only led to new heights from this not so common approach of his. It was as if he couldn't get enough of me.

William's tongue was deep within my mouth. At one point I thought I may choke on him. I slowly stripped my man. We were still at the front door. I caressed his neck, slightly nibbling at his ear lobe and slowly worked my way down to his very excited erect cock. William was now standing stark bollock naked in front of me and I was on my knees in just my knickers.

William removed my dressing gown before I had even started to strip him, which now lay crumpled up behind us acting as a future cushion. I devoured his hardness. William was soon at the point where he knew if he did not remove himself from my warm, wet, moist, mouth he would explode and he did not want that, not yet anyway. William wanted to feel my tight pussy. He pulled me up to him and then pushed me back on the stairs and fucked me deep and slow and then hard and fast until we both came together.

I knew nothing of William's evening as of yet. William had been far too tense to talk let alone expose what he had been involved with that evening. However, William was totally relaxed now and knew that he had needed sex, well sex with me, to allow himself some sort of sanity after his day.

We were lying in bed, baby Marcus was sound asleep. William had been totally honest with me about his whereabouts that evening. I was relishing in the avenging of Sadie's predator when William then dropped the bombshell that he in his moment of insane sadistic sanity had accidentally referred to himself as having a daughter in front of Frankie. Although he was sure he didn't mention Sadie he couldn't be a hundred percent.

It felt like my stomach had dropped through to the kitchen that was beneath my bedroom right now. The head spin that I felt from the thought of Frankie knowing the truth made me feel drunk and extremely disorientated. I knew that Frankie would go psychopathic crazy. The fact that baby Marcus wasn't even brought up at least allowed me a little hope as if Frank knew this she would be convinced that me and William had been having an affair for the last fifteen years, which clearly was so far from the truth, and then Frank would be one dangerous lady on a war path, heading in my direction. I knew that I had to face Frankie and tell her the whole truth but William was not allowing that.

'There is no way you are going anywhere near her, she is one dinlo cunt and believe me, Kate, the girl has a warped side and you my darling are not getting in an inch of her line of fire.' William was not budging on his decision and I felt this from his blunt harsh tone.

Although I was elated by William being protective of me, I knew that as a neighbour and friend, I at least owed Frankie my version of events. It was early hours before I managed to allow myself the pleasure of sleep. But as quickly as I had found this moment of peace, baby Marcus was stirring. I decided to take myself and the baby downstairs to give him his bottle. I didn't want to disturb William, he looked dead to the world. As I approached the door to the landing I could smell burning and when I opened the bedroom door, the smoke was unbearable.

'Will ... Will ... Fuck, Will, wake up!' I was frantically screaming at him through bouts of choking and coughing.

William jumped up startled and shouted. 'Shit what?!' Then he too saw the smoke. I was coughing hard and banged the door shut. I covered the baby over with his blanket, his cries were no longer hunger whimpers, they were crazed and high pitched with pure fear. It was like he sensed the sheer panic that was vibrating off me, invading into his tiny little body and that his cries were now an internal mirror image of his protector and provider's fear for the loss of their life. I looked at Will for help.

'What do we do?' I was panicking. My voice was wavering.

William's instinct kicked in. 'We get out the fucking window that's what we do!' With that, Will was smashing the window through with the bedside cabinet. 'Stand back, Kate!' William shouted at me. Then he was launching the mattress through. 'You hold onto me, I will hang you as far

down as possible and then jump onto the mattress,'
William told me. He was now putting the duvet over the
broken shards of glass that were left cemented into the
frame. He then gently lifted me and baby Marcus out of the
window. I held onto William's arm for dear life and
squeezed my baby so tight for fear of losing his life. I could
see the wild-like flames through the kitchen window as I
skimmed past with baby Marcus, and in that moment it all
felt too surreal and like that of a tragic movie scene rather
than my life.

I was now sitting on the mattress that me and William
had just minutes ago been lying peacefully in. The irony
pained me, and now slightly discombobulated I watched
William jump from the bedroom window down to safety.
We were all now huddled on the mattress half naked,
paused in a moment of a smoke dazed semi-reality. The
noise and the brightness of the fire appeared to have
woken my neighbours who, it seemed, had already called
the emergency services which were heard in the near
distance. Derrick, the old man who lived next door to me
had brought some blankets out and gave them to us, which
allowed us some dignity in the chaos that had managed to
lay us bare for all to see. My milk had dried up the last
couple of weeks and I desperately needed a bottle for the
baby. He was screaming merry hell. Another neighbour
who lived about five doors up had a newborn, she too
came to mine and baby Marcus's rescue.

The ambulance arrived and checked us all over. We were lucky, the crew had said. It took three fire engines to tackle the blaze and put the fire out. The house was left looking like a black, smoke-filled skeleton. The police were asking all sorts of questions. Apparently, they had found a petrol jerry can at the back door therefore it would appear that someone had a vendetta against us and that someone had intended to start the fire rather than it be an accident.

I was furious. I knew there was only one person that would be so sick to do something like this. Frankie fucking Twirp. I was not holding back in telling the police. However William was not so quick at pointing the finger. I think he was worried what Frankie would throw back at him. Why he worried I don't know, as if she would open her big, fat, dirty cunt of a mouth about the remnants of the gruesome gynaecologist she wouldn't only put William up for murder she would also drag Tom and her silly self down with him. Frankie was loose and unpredictable but not stupid enough to dig herself a bigger fucking hole. To be honest I think jail would be a safer place for Frankie Twirp right now as I don't think William will take it lightly that she may have just tried to kill his own flesh and blood. William was already on the phone, he borrowed old man Derrick's as both of ours were most definitely disintegrated, along with the rest of my home, I solemnly thought. The overwhelming feeling of abandonment washed through me to the point my whole body was physically shaking. I think it must be the shock or the actual reality of the sorry

situation unfolding itself before my very own eyes, it was
the fact that we should have been in there fried to a crisp.
That thought alone made my blood run cold. I held my
baby closer as if he was my saviour. It's him, my baby blue,
who really is keeping me standing right now and not falling
into a pathetic trembling heap on the floor. Within the next
fifteen minutes a red Mercedes with blacked-out windows
pulled up. I recognised the car instantly. I had wondered
for a very long time who it was that drove this shiny, bright
red, blacked-out, flashy vehicle and now it seems as though
tragedy will be the reason behind my finally meeting
William's mystery driver.

# Forty-One

The day got shockingly worse. William and I arrived back at William's apartment with baby Marcus and whilst William was in the shower there was a knock at the door. It was the police. I shouted to William that the police were there and wanted to speak with him.

William's first thought was that Frankie had opened her mouth up to them and here they were now to arrest him. We were not prepared for what the police were about to tell us. They asked us to sit down. They explained that there had been three fires that morning and they believed that they were all connected.

'As you are already aware the first fire was your home, Miss Andrews. The second was your garage, Mr White. We have also informed your business partner Tom Crane of this. And the third was at the address of Miss Frankie Twirp. Mr White, I am so sorry to have to inform you there were fatalities. Miss Twirp died on her way to hospital and your youngest son Josh White was dead by the time the emergency services got to him. Your son John White is at the hospital in a critical condition. We would urge you to go and see him as soon as possible, Mr White. Again we are extremely sorry for your loss however, as hard as this must be for you we need you to identify your son, Mr White. I will leave my contact details here. Please can you call me later today so we can arrange this? Thank you, we will leave you now.' Then the two officers left.

William sat in silence. I tried to comfort him. However, William did not respond to my affectionate advances, instead he pulled a tracksuit on and put his trainers on, threw a phone at me and said he would call, then he left.

I was now alone, so alone. Although I had a phone I had no contact numbers and no car to get anywhere. My car was fine but my car keys were lost in the fire. All I could do was cry. Those poor babies. Visions of baby Josh cremated made my body physically shake. I felt so much guilt. Guilt for Sadie, guilt for William, guilt for Frankie and those poor innocent boys. Frankie must've started the fire by accident. I could not comprehend Frankie's state of mind, to burn herself and her two precious babies alive, Frankie had completely lost the plot.

I decided to get a cab to Fiona's, at least I could get Jack's number and contact Sadie and Laney. Although the thought of seeing the tragedy that lay at my late neighbour's home only made me feel sick like I had effectively been the cause of Frankie's mental breakdown, and now her and William's son's death was all that I could think of. How did it all come to this, I thought?

Fiona was a mess. Death was all she could smell. Fiona could barely talk. I had never seen the woman so broken, not even when Scarlett, her daughter, fucked off with Fiona's old man.

'Oh babe, I saw the baby. Black and limp he was!' Fiona was an emotional wreck and who could blame her, anyone who witnessed a dead baby would be the same.

'Fiona please listen to me, It's absolutely tragic and I too nearly lost me and baby Marcus earlier, Frankie started a fire at my place too.' I didn't really know what to say.

'Why? What do you mean? Why would she do this, Kate?' Fiona was confused and begging for answers. I knew I owed the lady that sat before me the truth. Yet I was so scared of any more rejection I hesitated in my response.

'I ... I don't know Fi. I ... I ... I'm so sorry it's my fault, it's all my fucking fault. I've made such a mess of so many lives!' I was now crying with Fiona.

'It's not your fault, you silly cow, you didn't start no fires!' cried Fiona.

'No I may not have started them Fi, but I certainly was the fuel!' I looked at Fiona. 'I had an affair with William fifteen years ago, Fi. And Sadie is his daughter and Frank found out last night, hence the fires she started.' I said the latter at speed.

Fiona was open-mouthed and stunned. 'You got to be joking me. Seriously I can't fucking believe it. Kate you, honest Kate! No way!'

'I'm sorry Fiona, it's true,' I quietly apologised.

'Well it's still not your fault. You fucked up, yes, but you didn't kill anyone and you were obviously young! And does

Sadie know, Kate?' Fiona, although shocked at my honesty, could still see that it was naivety that brought me my past and would forgive any girl that.

'She does now, only a couple of days ago. That's why she's staying at Laney's, Fi. It's all such a mess. But can I tell you one good thing, Fi?' I sounded gutted even though I was about to divulge my innermost wicked revenge.

'Go on!' Fiona prompted my positive tale.

'Well, William and Tom got the nonce that molested Sadie. Butchered him apparently. That was how Frank found out about Sadie being William's.' I had no emotion when I told Fiona.

'Tom didn't say anything! Kate, he was more concerned about the garage!' Fiona sounded shocked that her son hadn't informed her of his avenge for Sadie.

'The garage was planned, Fi. Evidence etc. Frank had no part in that one! Just mine and her house. Tom probably isn't even aware of the fire at my house, Fi.' I informed Fiona.

'Well when I spoke with him, he was assisting the police with their enquiries. He was aware of next door only because I told him. I don't know how he will take it when he learns Frank is dead.' The tears sprang to Fiona's eyes and she felt a lump rise in her throat as she mentioned Frankie being dead.

I was also crying, I couldn't believe that both Frankie and baby Josh were gone. The shame I felt for my part in this was breathtaking. The fact was, I knew I didn't start those fires. But I did know in my heart they were only started because of myself and my own debauchery. Would William ever forgive this? His baby boy dead and his other son fighting for his life. The physical pain I felt for William's loss was so potent I could not eat or drink since I had learnt of the deaths. Nothing would go down not even a coffee. I yearned to be near William right now and support his pain.

There was a knock at Fiona's door. It was Sadie and Laney all panicked and overwhelmed with what they had heard on the news and just seen next door. I could hear their worried voices from the kitchen. I just couldn't lift myself from the seat, not even to reassure Sadie I was fine and here. My own voice seemed to freeze. As soon as Sadie saw me she ran at me, screaming,

'Thank God! Oh, Mum, I thought you were gone!' Sadie was really quite emotional. I was pleased she was now showing some care towards me but still I couldn't find it in me to talk. I could only lean my head into my daughter's arms. What could I say? It was so bad.

# Forty-Two

It was three weeks before I heard anything from William. I had no contact number for him and could only rely on him to call me. We were all staying with Laney as obviously there was nowhere else to stay.

Sadie had been a great support and our relationship was certainly on the mend. Jack had told Sadie about the attack of her perpetrator and therefore Sadie had since warmed to the thought of William White being her father. One bonus, I thought. Sadie was well aware her relationship with William would not be that of a sweet girly dream but a realistic real relationship with her alive and kicking biological father. The police had not found the father of baby Kate, good old DI Duddin popped to Laney's to inform them they were still searching but had no news at this present time.

Let's hope they don't come across the half-dead nonce, I thought. I was bathing baby Marcus when my phone started ringing. I ignored it as rushing to pick it up whilst in the middle of water, bubbles and baby was pointless. I knew it would ring off by the time I Krypton Factored my way to it, so left it to buzz away. However, I could have kicked myself when I realised it had been William, he left me a voicemail.

'Kate. Kate, it's me Will. I'm sorry babe, really fucking sorry. He's gone, Kate. John Boy's gone. I will be in contact just give me some time!' 'That was it. Yet again I am waiting. Yes it is tragic but to just keep rejecting me and his living kids makes me feel slightly fucking sick!

'I'm a cunt, ain't I, Lane? But I just can't help the way I feel. I'm devastated for him and want so much to be near him and comfort him but no I'm not allowed. What the fuck is that all about, Lane?' I was sounding off to my friend. Laney was trying to empathise with me but sounded quite harsh.

'Time, Kate, fuck, give the bloke time. He has had the most shocking year! I know you want him to need you, but sometimes people don't need people they need time, time alone. Fuck I would know this, Kate! Have you ever dealt with death? No.'

'Fuck, Lane, talk about write me off. No, you're right. I haven't had to deal with death like some of you have! But fuck, girl, I've had the worst year ever!' I was offended by Laney's response.

'Babe, stop it. Yes your year has been one to remember but may I say you my dear friend are walking away with two beautiful healthy children. William although he has gained two children he has also tragically lost two and well the other as we know is a shameful write off, Kate!' Laney was so fair and caring and this was highlighted to me in her reply.

It was then that we were interrupted by the doorbell ringing. It was William's mother, Rose White. God, I hadn't seen Rose in years, her and Frankie never saw eye-to-eye so she never went to Frankie's. William would always visit his mother and now here she was at Laney's front door. It was like looking at Sadie in forty years' time. An elegant, classy lady was Rose White. I had forgotten how low and delicate her voice was.

'Hello dear. It's Rose, William's mother, he has asked me to come and see you.' She spoke so softly she managed to relax me instantly. Laney was busying herself and offering refreshments. Rose walked straight over to baby Marcus who was sitting in his bouncer. 'May I?' Rose was leaning down to pick her grandson up.

I looked at her with a smile and replied, 'Of course please do.' I felt tears falling from me. I knew she knew he was hers from the way she nuzzled her nose into him to breathe him in. Rose too had tears in her eyes.

Rose looked at me and said, 'William came to see me this morning after we lost John Boy.' The immaculate woman that stood before me had to take a breath to discourage her own voice from breaking. 'Kate, my son says he loves you. But for now he must leave.'

I felt myself crumble. My own emotions were beating me right now. I managed, 'What do you mean? He is leaving!' My own words seemed jumbled. My brain was jumbled.

His mother is telling me he loves me but he is leaving me. 'What the fuck? Sorry Rose for my language.' I felt Rose didn't take too kindly to my common manner and had to apologise. Was this because I wanted so much for her acceptance of us too?

Sadie after all was her only granddaughter, closest thing she would get to a daughter and maybe she already hates me for that or because I have literally just played the murderer in her family's life.

'Kate, I know this is not what you wanted to hear but William is my priority. He also told me to give you his keys to the apartment at the Dock Yard and there's twenty thousand in cash to see you over. If at any point you need anything please call me. I will leave you my contact details, Kate.' Rose spoke with authority and handed me a black briefcase full of bank notes. I was stunned into silence.

Rose quickly drank her coffee and departed. However, she made it clear before she left that she would very much like a relationship with both her grandchildren and advised me to make plans for this and contact her. She reinforced the fact she was available whenever was convenient. The woman was so intense, she reminded me of a Greek goddess who spoke volumes. I guess I should be thankful. At least my children now had a paternal grandmother that gave a fuck even if their father didn't.

*TO BE CONTINUED ...*

Printed in Great Britain
by Amazon